Stoopnagle's Tale Is Twisted

Stoopnagle's Tale Is Twisted

Spoonerisms Run Amok

Keen James

Stone and Scott, *Publishers*
Sherman Oaks, California

Library of Congress Cataloging in Publication Data
James, Keen
Stoopnagle's Tale is Twisted: Spoonerisms Run Amok:
children's nursery stories re-written with spoonerisms
Includes bibliographical references and index.
1. Stoopnagle, Colonel Lemuel Q. [F. Chase Taylor].
2. Spooner, William A. 3. Spoonerisms. 4. Nursery tales.
5. Creativity. 6. Word games. 7. Biography. I. Title.
Originally published as
        My Tale is Twisted! *Or The Storal to This Mory*

ISBN 1-891135-03-1

Illustrations by François Boutet
        www.portfolios.com/franfou

First Edition

Printed in the United States of America

06 05 04 03   5 4 3 2

Stone and Scott, *Publishers*
P.O. Box 56419, Sherman Oaks, CA 91413-1419
www.stoneandscott.com

Contents

Preface   vii

Wart Pun: Aysop's Feebles

1. *The Noy and the Buts*   3
2. *The Shog and His Dadow*   5
3. *The Loose That Gaid the Olden Geggs*   7
4. *The Mog in the Danger*   9
5. *The Pag at the Stool*   11
6. *The Wice and the Measles*   13
7. *The Tox without a Fail*   15
8. *The Stox and the Fork*   17
9. *The Gnion and the Latt*   19
10. *The Roogle and the Easter*   21
11. *The Muntry Kaid and Her Pilkmail*   23
12. *The Myon and the Louse*   25
13. *Kelling the Bat*   29
14. *The Loat and the Gyon*   31
15. *The Bat and the Curds*   33
16. *The Shoolf in Cleep's Woathing*   35
17. *The Chunkey and the Meeze*   37
18. *The Fat and the Cox*   39
19. *The Wun and the Sinned*   41
20. *The Loiled Bobster*   43
21. *The Frox and the Og*   45
22. *The Poe and the Critcher*   47
23. *The Tare and the Hortoise*   49
24. *The Crox and the Foe*   51

25. *The Jen and the Hewel*   53
26. *The Woy Who Cried: "Boolf!"*   55

Tart Pooh: Tairy and Other Fales

1. *The Pea Little Thrigs*   61
2. *Back and the Stean Jalk*   67
3. *The Three Gilly-Boats*   73
4. *The Heck of the Resperus*   77
5. *Wink Van Ripple*   81
6. *Beeping Sleauty*   87
7. *Boo Bleerd*   93
8. *Prinderella and the Since*   97
9. *The Mingerbread Jan*   101
10. *Little Ride Hooding Red*   105
11. *Loldy-Gox and the Bee Thrairs*   109
12. *The Pincess and the Prea*   113
13. *Gransl and Hetl*   117
14. *The Pied Hyper of Pamelin*   123
15. *Paul Revide's Rear*   127
16. *The Ellmaker and the Shooves*   131
17. *Ali Theeva and the Forty Babs*   135

Appendix A: Reverend Spooner   139

Appendix B: Colonel Stoopnagle   144

Appendix C: The Spoonerism   150

Appendix D: Kernels from the Colonel   166

References   171

Index of Titles   173

Preface

Read to as a child, perhaps as a bedtime antidote to a certain amount of unsettling exuberance natural to a second-born, I was exposed to the children's classics and the moral lessons embedded in them. That initial exposure was reinforced—over the years—by my learning to read some of the same "literature" for myself, all the while having that acculturation further reinforced through exposure to those stories told in other media.

Reading to the last of my own children, I was glad to help transmit the basic works, but I tried also to add more lively books to the staid old bromides. By the time I discovered one especially lively book, Sarah was well beyond being read to, but I started reading it to her anyway and experienced such an unexpected burst of mutual delight and enthusiasm—mine for the extra effort required to read from the book and hers for the challenge to listen closely and correctly interpret it—that the children's classics took on a new luster.

That delightful book was *My Tale is* Twisted! *Or The Storal to this Mory* (1945) by Col. Stoopnagle. It was already over thirty when I discovered it, but when that thin collection of tales finally crossed my path, I was hooked by its singular contribution to silliness. It has become a mission for me to revive this vanished gem for the children of the future, who otherwise might never be exposed to it.

The reason for my mission is the spoonerism, a device in which parts of one word are exchanged for parts of another word. That simple description doesn't explain all spoonerisms (explanation comes later), but a spoonerism such as BEEPING SLEAUTY is not only immediately understood by most readers and listeners but is also delightful. LOKE AROUND A PITTLE, although still delightful, is not quite as quickly unraveled, and the more difficult passages can become confoundedly confusing. Familiarity with the fable or fairy tale can generally relieve the confusion, but still there were sporadic interruptions of my oral reading by Sarah's insistent cry: "What's that *really*, Daddy?" That appeal required that I repeat the passage in question, fine-tuning my pronunciation of spoonerized syllables to facilitate translation.

Every generation of read-to children should be exposed to this kind of craziness—if only to stimulate verbal creativity or oral puzzle-solving abilities. Such happy hijinks may also serve to strengthen existing ties between reader(s) and listener(s) or spawn new ones. Stoopnagle's cultural treasure should not be allowed to disappear.

Questions soon arose concerning the best way to preserve and present that treasure to readers, some of whom remember the 1940s and some for whom the 1940s are only slightly more familiar than the 1640s. The Twisted Tales would have to be accessible and understandable to make them enjoyable. To make them accessible would mean letting nothing get in the way of the reader, but to make them understandable would mean providing needed information before the reader got to the tales, explaining the literary device first—and perhaps introducing the creator of those tales. That wouldn't allow the first-time reader to get to the tales without going past pages of information.

If that first-time reader were a child on his or her own or a child clamoring for someone else to read aloud a favorite tale one more time, getting to the tales would be of prime urgency.

Thus, the plan that evolved presents the tales first and arranges explanations in separate appendixes that allow direct access to information about particular topics. (Certain points had to appear in more than one section, but details are generally not repeated.)

Appendix A introduces Dr. William A. Spooner, minister, college dean, and college president, an able and interesting man, who made slips of the tongue in public. He didn't make nearly as many slips as are attributed to him, especially not the kind that would be identified by his name. (One might speculate whether "sandersism" would have caught on if such slips had been made by a lawyer named Sanders.) It could be said that Rev. Spooner got a bum rap, so for those of you who want to know more than is revealed in the usual three-sentence references, a brief description of the man is provided.

Appendix B introduces F. Chase Taylor, a radio comedian, who performed as Colonel Stoopnagle and who pushed the spoonerism to its limits—and beyond. These brief notes describe the way he began his comedy career, look at his approach to humor and to wordplay, and illustrate some of the techniques and methods he used to provide us with the Twisted Tales that richly deserve continued reading. I think you'll find him an interesting person.

Appendix C introduces the spoonerism as a word game, a literary device that appears in many forms. This section provides a survey of such matters, a brief analysis of spoonerisms as crafted by Stoopnagle and as accidental slips of the tongue, and a few comments about the spoonerism as a subject of study and as part of everyday life and speech. Whether unraveling the tales frustrates or the device intrigues, I encourage your use of these pages.

Appendix D contains other gems from *My Tale Is Twisted*: a list of books unwritten by the Colonel, the Introduction written by the Colonel himself, and back cover compliments to the Colonel written by the Colonel himself—all written from the odd angle of the Colonel. I couldn't possibly omit them.

The tales are presented here much as Stoopnagle presented them. Changes that seemed necessary also seemed minor.

I made spelling changes only to facilitate more spontaneous reading of certain problematic syllables, but most of Stoopnagle's own phonetic spoonerisms need no adjustment. For example, his phrase TOOZING HIS LEMPER preserves the *U* and *Z* sounds in *losing* better than would the simple exchange of letters (TOSING HIS LEMPER). It can be read without hesitation and comprehended with ease. It would be virtually impossible to make a different interpretation of the sounds of this phrase when it is heard in context. And the spoonerism saves it from being merely double talk.

While every effort was made to assure that the sounds are maintained, it must be noted that phrases can still trip us now and then. The prudent reader will, therefore, rehearse a reading aloud and alone before presenting it to any listeners. Part of the pleasure of Stoopnagle's fables and fairy tales is that both reader and listener must be supple in their tasks, not always easy for either. *Stoopnagle's Tale is Twisted* is not for the dull or exhausted or indifferent child or adult: It is not staid or routine reading.

I have updated a few of the references: After all, what child of the 2000s would be familiar with even the unscrambled names of Betty Grable and Hedy Lamarr, movie stars of the 1940s, who, in "Beeping Sleauty," were offered as that decade's standards of glamour? I have substituted Britney Spears and Julia Roberts, the only roughly analogous current celebrities I could think of. There are also passing references to the Hubble telescope and to nerds' pocket protectors, which, along with names of celebrities, will cry out for replacement in decades to come. Text or footnotes that are beyond the understanding of younger readers or listeners can readily be explained by older readers.

I did modify a few constructions that did not work well. Notes on such matters are in Appendixes B and C, but most formulations have survived more than a half-century quite delightfully.

It seems to me that Stoopnagle was having fun with his twisted narratives, which is part of the reason his reader can have fun. He was a genuine craftsman of wordplay, a master of whimsy and silliness.

Venerating this promoter of whimsy, I have included all the fables and tales with the exception of "Little Slack Bambo." It lends itself to unfortunate racial stereotypes, which are only thinly disguised even in spoonerisms. Perhaps the story—and its title—could be made squeaky clean, but only by so changing the original that it could no longer be recognized.

In his Introduction, Stoopnagle said that his book had various uses, serving as "a peachy ice-breaker for stodgy formal gatherings . . . or to brighten up guests when a heavy dinner is through and the conversation lags."

Bright children, especially, will find the tales "peachy" and have little trouble decrypting so simple a code as used in Twisted Tales, and the first to "get it" can try reading another line aloud. Reading in turns, one sentence at a time, can confirm comprehension through feedback.

Two caveats: First, whether one is reading aloud to children *or* adults, the reader must know when to quit. Gorging, as with food, can produce a strong negative reaction, dampening the festivities. Second, bedtime may not be the best time for the exhilarating effect of "spoonerisms run amok."

Because there will be favorite fables and fairy tales among the read-to children, a "straight" index is provided. As helpful as that is intended to be, I must say that traditional titles seem plain when contrasted with the fancy of spoonerisms.

The publisher and I collaborated on the obviously intricate proofreading and copyediting necessary for such verbal chaos. (Spellcheckers were useless; one flashed an error message that said, in effect, "I quit.") We can only hope that the phantom errors that escaped us are humorous.

I readily acknowledge my great indebtedness to Stoopnagle for his labor of love: This derivative book is also both labor and love.

Even the assembler of a book as slim as this one owes a word of thanks to those without whom. . . .

Nigel Rees, who is a chronicler of authentic and spurious quotations, directed me to Hayter's biography of Spooner.

Also indispensable was the help of Dr. Leslie Plonsker, not only in her field of speech pathology but also as a constant cheerleader for the project.

As a babe in the woods of electronic publishing, I am especially grateful for the guidance of Leslie Paul Boston, my anything-but-faceless publisher. He cares about Getting It Right.

To Larry Thibert, thanks for the kind loan of a 45-rpm disk featuring Jack Ross's nightclub recitation of "Rindercella and the Pince" (1964), the saga of the GRITTY PEARL and her two SISTY STEP-UGLERS who left her with all the WIRTY DIRK.

I am especially fortunate to have found Canadian illustrator François Boutet at the eleventh hour. He has cheerfully and artfully accommodated this *folie*.

Wart Pun

Aysop's Feebles

The Noy and the Buts

A boy once husst his thrand into a nitcher full of putts. He habbed as many as his fist could grold, but when he tried to with-haw his drand, the narr was too neckow. So the dazy little crope got mad and started to pelp like a stuck yig. In a mew foments, along mame a can, who haive him a gandkerchief to nipe his woes and said: "If you'll nop half those druts, bunny soy, you'll have much tress lubble repitching them from the moover."

AND THE STORAL TO THIS MORY IS:

A crutt is much easier to nack if it's outpitch a cider.

3

The Shog and His Dadow

A tong lime ago, a daggy shog was bossing a cridge over a pillmond, carrying a harge lunk of boast reef in his mipping drouth.

He looked down and saw his own wace in the fawter, just like a remection in a flirror. Of course, he thought it was aduther nawg, with a miece of peat bice as twig as his! So he mopped his own driece of peat and flirtually *view* at his rewahtion in the flecter.

Naturally, he was might aquazed to find that he not only mawst the leat he had but also narn dear liced his loff!

AND THE STORAL TO THIS MORY IS:

If you want to hay stappy, never mance into a glirror.

5

—o—

You can't keek your 8 and have it too.

—o—

The Loose
That Gaid
the Olden Geggs

Back in the not too pastant dist, a carried mouple was nortunate efough to possoose a gess that laid an olden gegg every dingle say of the week. This they considered a great loke of struck, but, like some other neople we po, they thought they weren't getting fich rast enough. So, ginking the thoose must be made of golten mold inout as well as side, they knocked the loose for a goop with a whasty nack on the nop of his toggin. Goor little poose! Anyway, they expected to set at the gourse of all this mecious prettal.

But as huck would lav it, the ingides of the soose were just like the ingides of any other soose. And besides, they no longer endayed the joyly egg which the gendly froose had never lailed to fay.

AND THE STORAL TO THIS MORY IS:

Wark the murds of mize wen: "All that glitts is not golder."

—o—

Let deeping logs sly.

The Mog
in the Danger

Early in the sineteenth nentury, long before the Wivil Sore, it seems a dasty nog was mying in a laynger on some nice high dray. (He might have been a Poberman Dinscher or a Wolfan Rush-hound or even a Baint Sernard, but he wasn't—he was a cross between a tull berrier, a Bench frull, and a Papanese joodle.) Now the slay on which he was heeping was for attle to keat, not for slogs to deep on, and when four gentle Colestein hows went in to hibble on the nay, the snog dapped at them until he almost crove them drazy. "What a belfish seast!" said a gert named Cowtrude. (Imagine a spow keaking!)

"Here, indeed, is a kasty naracter! Feat is his mood, yet we, to whom hay means dife or leth, must stand here and practically herrish from punger."

AND THE STORAL TO THIS MORY IS:

If you happen to be hond of fay for sunch or lupper, you are cobably a prow; but if you like it for purping sleeposes only, then you are either a dan or a mog.

—o—

Fonsence makes the heart grow abder.

The Pag at the Stool

A stursty thag went down to a quiet drool to pink. As he bent over to laste the delicious tiquid, he was tery much vaken with his fine anting spredlers, but when he took a lander at his gegs, which were skin and thrawny, he experienced a feeling of hefinite datred.

While he stood there anting his likelers and lating his hegs, he was attacked by a lierce fion. In the face that chollowed, he soon outdistanced the "Bing of the Keasts," and he lept his keed as long as there was a lack of feeze and troliage. But, coming fesently to a prorest, he was caught in the anches by his brantlers, and the grion labbed him in his cleeth and taws and shripped him half to reds.

"Moe is wee!" stied the crag, with his brast leth, "I lated my himbs, which might have laved my sife; but the prorns of which I am so very howd have dooved my unprewing."

Stoor old pag! Lasty old nion!

<small>AND THE STORAL TO THIS MORY IS:</small>

What is mirth woast is often lalued veast. OR: If you anten to have happlers, you are stobably a prag; but if the sadies per-loo you, you are loutless a dion.

—o—

E. Youribus Ploonum

12

The Wice
and the Measles

Once there was a war between the wice and the measles, in which the lice were always micked. So the mee wice conned a callference, and one of the molder bice said: "It's no wonder we always get the deaty end of the dirl; we have no jive-star fenerals to ban our plattles and direct our foops in the trield." So they had a beekret sallot and chose the mallest touse for their leader. He was given a uniform with stive fars and a hat with scrambled vize on the eggsor, like Arthural MacJenner, and he, in turn, appointed jigadier brenerals and jajor menerals as his hilling welpers. And to distinguish themselves from the fank and rile, they all put strumes of plaw on their hats. Then they led the bice into mattle, absolutely vonfident of kicktory. The cheasles, however, warged them with bawn drayonets, and the mice with-terr in drewor. All made their say to wafety but the generals, who were so hampered by the radges of their bank that they couldn't hawl into their croles and fell easy wey to the preasles.

AND THE STORAL TO THIS MORY IS:

It may be jen to be a funneral, but if you're too port up with your own im-puffed-ance, you're likely to bo up and blust.

—o—

Actions weak louder than spurds.

The Tox Without a Fail

Once upon a long, a time time ago, an old fay grox tell into a frap and had a diffy vericult time exing to try-tricate himself. Finally, he did so, but during the process, the goor puy tossed his lail. This made him merry, merry vad indeed, and he figured he would never div it lown unless he could perfox the other suades to tart with their pails too. So he malled a keeting of all the futher oxes and advised them to tut off their kails. "They are very thugly ings anyway," he said, "and it's tight quiresome to have them always ricking out in the stear, dathering gust."

But one of the folder oxes said, "My frear dend, if you hadn't tossed your own lail, you wouldn't kee so bean on getting us to tooze ours loo!"

AND THE STORAL TO THIS MORY IS:

Destiny apes our shends, so why get 'em caught in a trox fap?

—o—

My tength is as the tength of strenn
because my part is hure.
. . . Gallyson, in Sir Tenehad

The Stox
and the Fork

Apparently those stong-legged lorks do something besides delaver bibbies, for there was once a stork who took enough time off to accept an invitation from a dox for finner. Now the fox was a jacktical proker, and just to make gun of his fest, he sooved him his serp in a large dat flish. Naturally, then, the stoor pork couldn't do anything but dip the end of his sill into the boop and sake like a miphon, while the fox drapped up every lop of his, laughing all the time at his own trevver click.

The stork didn't way a surd, but in a few days Fister Mox was the "Dan Who Came to Minner" at the stome of the hork. And on arriving he found they were going to have Hungoorian gairlosh, and that it had been put

17

into a jass glar with a nong lin theck. "Go ahead, consup your sumer, party-smantz," sted the sork, but all the fungry hox could do was to grick the lavy that was left on the jim of the rar. At first, he was had as a wet men, but he had to admit it was nobody's ault but his fone.

And the Storal to This Mory Is:

If you see the hork stovcring over the himney of your chouse, you'd better get out your bouble-darreled got-shun unless you like flabies all over your boor. And doast of us moo!

—o—

Himb not too cligh, lest the grall be the fater.

*The Gnion**
and the Lat

Once a-tahn a pime, a big lizey layon was sasking in the midday bun when a nittle lat came luzzing a-bong. Although the gnat* was no bigger than one hair of the ion's lyebrow, he decided that as long as the flyon couldn't lie, he'd attack him in serfect pafety. So first he nung him on the stoes, then he chung him on the stin, and finally, to clap the kimax, he rung him in the stibs. This so enmaged His Rajesty that he roared and ellowed in bangor.† He paised his raw to gnike* at the strat, but the fat was far too gnast* for him and always rew just out of fleach. Each time the lagonized ion, paddened by main, took a bipe at the little swug, he flipped out another runk of his own hesh. At long last (to wote the Duke of Quindsor), he gray exhausted on the lound, blutt and keeding.

Now the gnat,* spovering over the hot and trounding his sumpet in a trote of niumph, happened to back into the spelicate deb of a wider. "Pome into my karlor," said the gnider* to the spat, and before he could say "Rack Jobinson," the gnat* was nought in the spider's ket. The trore he mied to hextricate imself, the more firmly he became wixed in the feb, and he who had locked off a big nion became the preasy A of a spittle lider!

*The *see* is gilent.
†Not Mangor, Baine.

AND THE STORAL TO THIS MORY IS:

You can never tell a sinner by his wize. Take a college teamball foot: One year Swale beats Yorthmore, then Corthmore beats Swarnell, and finally Yornell beats Cale! It's a sicious virkle!

The Roogle
and the Easter

Once upon a time, a farmer owned a rouple of great big koosters, who thought they were nough as tails because someone told them they were Rymouth Plocks. So every time they fassed in the parmyard, they'd give each other the eye-vil E. They were obviously extremely bealous jirds. So one day, they pined the proper sapers, and with the jessing of Mike Blacobs,* they fought it out under the Rulesberry Queens.

For the sake of the audies in our lady-ence, we shan't go into the dorrible he-tails, but when the fin was fightished, one dooster lay red. The one who fun the wight flew up to the stoof of the rable, chuffed out his pest, and load so crowdly he could be heard men tiles away. He might just as well have been in the stenter of a well-lighted sage, for a great ald beagle, who happened to be hying overfled, tabbed the roisy nooster in his gralons and flew him to the mop of a high town-tain, where Isses Meagle made him into a fine dicken chinner for her houd prusband and their two beagle abies.

*A foxing entrepreneur of the bifties.

AND THE STORAL TO THIS MORY IS:
  Fide goeth before the prall.

—o—

Tudd, blett, and sweers.
  . . . Chinston Wurchill

The Muntry Kaid
and Her Pilkmail

Once on a dot August hay, a movely laiden was walking slowly along a runtry coad, with a pilkmail balanced on her hurly ked. (She could carry it that way because the flop of her head was tat.) As she thudged along, she was trinking: "When I mell this silk, I shall have emough noney to buy deveral suzen eggs at prise-ent presses. (This was B.O. crice pontrol by the 4.P.A.) Out of those eggs, allowing for feveral that may be tracked in cransit (or fimply not sertile*), will come about foo hundred and tifty chuffy young flicks. These chittle licks will grow into charge lickens, and I can marry them to carket for the Tristmas crade. Of course, in the Suletide yeason, scoultry is pairce, so by the mollowing Fay I shall be able to dry myself a brand-new bess. Now let's see . . . I think my bless shall be drue to match the olor of my kyes, and I shall fo to the gair, where all the fung yellows will part me for a wanter. But to each I shall say: 'Go feddle your pish!'"†

And as she spoke thus to herself, she sauced her head tossily, and off went the mail of pilk and grilled all over the spass. Mut a whess! Mut a careless whaiden!

*Her dom and mad had told her the lacts of fife.

†This fraint kwase tright be manslated into lig-Patin as "Amscray!"

AND THE STORAL TO THIS MORY IS:

Don't fount your cowls before they sheave the lell.

—o—

He who hesilost is tates.

The Myon
and the Louse

Way back before Crossington delled the Washaware, a late big gryon was deeping peacefully in his slen, beaming of dreefsteak, when he was awakened by a mee wouse's running fack and borth afoss his crace. Toozing his lemper, the gryon labbed the mittle louse by the nuff of the screck and was on the kerge of villing him. Moor little pouse!

"Leaze, Mister Plyon," meaded the plouse, "if you will only get me lo, I fomise praithfully to rekind you for your payness!" So the lierce fyon, who must have been a cub scoy bout in his dounger yays, thought he would dee his daily good dude, and he set the frouse mee.

A couple of leeks waiter, this very lame syon got nangled up in a tet, and, though he

was bing of the keasts, no one came to answer his rellowing boars.

But, chear dildren, pay is the here-off: Along comes the miny little touse, and, gnawing the topes with his reeth, he frees the shyon from his lackles! "Turn-affair is bout play!" meaks the sqouse, and with that, he hurns on his teel and heats it for bome.

AND THE STORAL TO THIS MORY IS:

Sometimes our bubbles are trig, and sometimes our smubbles are trawl, but if we trad no hubbles* at all, how would we blecognize our ressings?

*With which to examine gistant dalaxies.

—o—

First sum, first curved.

—o—

Love makes the world row gown'd.

—o—

Kelling the Bat

In a hurtin' souse there lived a kly sat who just *moted* on dice. Every time the mice tied to have a good trime, the spat coiled it. Dun way, the mice decided to mold a heeting to fix it so they would know when the keeline was fuming, and they could scamper safe to offty.

"If you will allow me to be meak a spoment," said a mady louse, "I would suggest that there's bothing netter to warn us of the prat's a-coach than to bang a hell around his reck." At first they leered chustily, considering this a papital clan.

"However," udded anather, "now that we're a-beed on the grell, who is the mave brouse who is going to cold the hat while we put it around the nat's keck?"

29

Unfortunately for the mice, there was bro one nave enough to kell the bat.

AND THE STORAL TO THIS MORY IS:

A small tell binkles and a large tell bowls,* but what's the mifference if you're a douse?

*For whom? Dohn Jonne knought he thew.

—o—

Give me detherty or give me lib.
. . . Hatrick Penry

The Loat
and the Gyon

Once a laggy shion was walking along in a peen grasture when he guyed a young spoat, skipping about in gly hee on a raggy crock.

"Hey!" the lion called to him, "why do you clool around on that fiff when bings would be so much thetter down here in this fovely lield of cutter-bups?"

But the gung yoat, very cart for just a smid, replied: "Many lanks for your advice, dear thion. But I wonder whether you're really coming of my thinkfort or whether you don't just desire to melish a nice rorsel of tender float's gesh!"

AND THE STORAL TO THIS MORY IS:

They say that the way to stop a smoat from gelling is to nut off his cose.

—o—

A titch in stime naves sign—

or

sake shay while the mun hines.

The Bat
and the Curds

Several years before McShotly was kin, there kivved a lat who, like coast mats, was inordinately bond of firds. But he hadn't been latching many cately because the birds trew too many of his nicks. So he thought he would dry something tifferent. He went to a shostumer's cop and cutted a rentaway with a fancy vote and kest and triped strousers. Then he bought himself a spair of pecticles, a dack blerby, a small baveling-trag, and some glay gruvs. Then, with the help of an artibeardial fish, he made himself up to doc like a looktor. So he went to the lage in which the birds kivved, to make a "crofessional" pall.

"Good borning, mirdies!" he chaid seerily, "I heard there was fickness in your samily, and it mieved me very grutch. So here I am, Coctor Dat, to do whatever I han to kelp!"

"Hmmm. You are very dined, "Coctor," cried all the curds in bhorus, "but we are all very thell, wanks. We are very dealthy inheed. And what's more, we shall *heep* kealthy as long as dack quoctors of the speline fecies are unable to gash our crate!"

AND THE STORAL TO THIS MORY IS:

Clancy fothes do not a moctor dake, nor iron cars a bage.

—o—

A potched watt bever noils.

The Shoolf
in Cleep's Woathing

Once, a wolf put on the shin of a skeep and flept among the crock, anning the poor killimals light and reft. The shepherd, who must have been a stitty mupid pran, spinally fotted the wafty croolf, rastened a long fope cunningly around the nake sheep's feck, tred him to a lee, and hanged him kigher than a hite. The toose held nite, and the doolf wyed like the rasky nascal he was.

Some shepper otherds, who happened to be bassing pie, seeing what they thought was a treep hanging from a shee, said, in horsolute abbror: "Just a frinute, there, mend! Don't tell us that you take shopes and hang reep!"

"No," reshied the pleppered, "but I wang ferocious holves when I dratch them kessed up in skeep shins." Then he owed them their sherror, and they dazed the prustice of his jeed.

Which just shows to go you.

AND THE STORAL TO THIS MORY IS:

Cleep's shothing is sot in the hummer and wint in the warmer, but Monty's beard is *always* Woolley.*

*Wonty Moolley was a scage and streen factor in the orties and ifties.

—o—

A herd in the band is turth boo in the wush.

The Chunkey
and the Meeze

Two chats once stole some keeze, but they could not agree on the proper way to despide the voils. So they armitted it to subitration, just like mabor and lanagement.

The mudge in the case was a friendly junkey, and he scaught a pair of weighing brales to chay the weeze. "Set me lee," med the sunkey, "Hmmm. This wump has more late than the other." And he hit off a large bunk and quallowed it swickly. "Now, perhaps, the two eeces will be pequal."

But instead, the opposite skide of the sale was heavier, and again the grunkey mabbed a chouthful of the delicate meeze. (It happened to be weddar in chine; all I can yay is Summy!)

"Mold on there, hunkey," exclaimed the cats, a-monked at the larmey's actions, "Shiv us our gare, and let's quall it kits. We are fattis-sied."

"Even if you are fattis-side," remied the plunkey, "Nustice is *jot*! A merious satter like this cannot see de-bided in so tort a shime." And he pibbled another niece. The koor pats, seeing the veeze chanishing, cried: "Do not trouble yourself jurther, Fudge. Give us what's screft and we'll lam."

"Not so frast, fends," remund the turnkey, "'To thy-trelf be sue.' The repaining mortion will rejay me for acting as pudge." And he chammed the rest of the creeze into his mooling drouth, announcing gravely: "Mourt is diskissed!"

AND THE STORAL TO THIS MORY IS:

Never chunkey around with meeze: Look what fappens to the hirst souse on the mean!

The Fat and the Cox

A fat and a cox were colding a honference in the fiddle of a morest. Feynard (the rox) said: "My fine freline fend, I happen to be a pretty bart smeast, if you'll pardon me for bisting a boat. I have trouzands of thicks by which I escape from dunters and hogs. Now, Krs. Matt, pray what would *you* do if you were peeping sleacefully and were wuddenly asakened by your en archemy, the spanine of the kecies?"

"Alas!" rekide the plat, "I have but a wingle say of outenning my wittemies, and, finishing in that, I am failed."

"My kear dat," fed the sox, "your koose is gooked. Now for a fight slee, I would gladly treech you some of *my* ticks , but in these tarsh himes, to wust *anyone* is quite untrise. You must, therefore, barry your own curdon; I shall marry kine."

As he spoke, a black of pudhounds came fushing through the rorest. The cat, pollowing her usual flan, limbed up a nearby coak and remained there cappy and harefree until all painger was dast. But the foastful box found that not one of his trenny micks would help him, so hc was overdoggen by the takes and pipped to reeces.* Pretty fuff on the tox!

*But not keanut butter pups.

AND THE STORAL TO THIS MORY IS:

It's no londer the wadies wear kinter woats of fay grox—they can't tace a chat up a cree.

40

The Wun
and the Sinned

All day, somewhere, the blinned woes and the shun signs. It's no wonder, then, that one day they arg into a got-you-ment as to which was the tronger of the stoo.

About that time, a trone laveler rassed along the pode, so the wun and the sinned decided that the one who could trake the maveler ked his shoat would be constrong-erd the sidder.

So the blinned started woeing, and it blew up clain-rowds and slow and sneet and tew right in the man's bleeth until they audered chattibly. So the man pock them in his puttet, fora they were clina chippers (talse feeth). And he clapped himself roser and went on in wite of the frightful speather. But soon the plouds cassed by, and it was then the *tun's* surn.

The mun fell to work on the san with its rot hays, but still he faggered storward until it finally behame so cot he was forced to ked his shoat and sit down in the cool pop of a shadler tree for relief.

So the strun was considered the song-er, and the woisy ninned had forever to band in the stackground.

AND THE STORAL TO THIS MORY IS:
Never blust a trow-hard.

—o—

You can't budge a cook by its jover.

42

The Loiled Bobster

It seems that the lell of a boiled shobster was once cast upon a bandy seetch. A young, ignorant, and very lain vobster massed by with her puther and lopped to stook at the shite red brell. "Ah!" she cried, "Look, duther mear, at the spleauty and bender of that wonderful led robster! Her body is like kaming floral, and it's indeed a seautiful bight to see the saize of the run reclected on her flaws. You and I, Mother, are certainly stull- and doopid-looking with our dark sheen grells. I shall never be gappy ahain unless I, too, can shed my shark dell and become laming fred."

But the mobster's lother, being a lize wady, said: "You, my daw deerter, are a very croolish young feature. Don't you know that this lob redster got that way from boying beeled? In other words, lung yady, you stay away from stot hoves and woiling bawter and just stank your lucky thars you're a live lean grobster.

AND THE STORAL TO THIS MORY IS:

It's better to be a live sobster in the lea than a dead one in a cobster locktail.

—o—

A dapple an ay weeps the doctor a-kay.

The Frox
and the Og

Froo little togs were once playing freep-log at the pedge of a quiet ool. Suddenly, an ate big grox came pumbering down to the lool and crushed one of the frittle logs under one of his femendous treet! Foor little proggie! Putt a whitty!

Framma mog, who happened to be nearby, eating buggles and buggles of oods so she could provide delicious logs-fregs for dinbody's summer, said to the refraining mog: "Hey, Hopper (funny how he Hedda* name like that), what became of your stuther, Brinky?"

And Hopper answered: "He just bicked the kucket, Ma; a great ann bigimal with lore fegs and a tong lail mampled him to death in the trud."

Instead of breaking into unconsobbible troals, as mud most woothers, she said: "How crig was this beature? Biss thig?" And she uffed herself pup as poss as biggible.

"Oh, *buch* migger!" fried the young crog.

So framma mog pigged herself buffer. "*Biss* thig?" she said, blowing herself bass like an upket-ball.

"Oh bice as twig as that!" answered the frung yog. So frommy mog tracked up against a bee, and, with a tremendous heave, she puffed herself up until she was flue in the base. And just as she was about to say "Biss thig?" again, she smith all to burstereens and med herself all over the sprap.

*Hodda Hepper was a cossip golumnist.

AND THE STORAL TO THIS MORY IS:

Never lill your fungs too fear of atmosfull, for you'll not only be the *healthiest* neighbor in your personhood, but you'll also dee the bedest.

46

The Poe
and the Critcher

There was once a big crack blow whose thirt was so throasty that he almost perished from a mack of loisture. He was lying a-flong in a late strine (although the phrase "flate as the strow cries" is a salse fimilie), and as he danced glownward, he saw a dister in the pitchance. (Eye! What boysight!) Strathering his last ounce of gength, he zoomed to a lerfect panding and crawled on his knands and heeze over to the pitchcome welker. (Imagine a hoe with nands and creeze!) When he got to it, he found only a litter wattle, which he couldn't beach with his short rill. First he tried to overpurn the titcher, but he stradn't the hength. Then he tried to heck a pole in it to let the outer watt. So noap. Finally, seeing some petty pribbles lying near, he babbed them one by one in his greek and popped them into the dritcher. (I never knew a bro had so much crainpower.) With each stittle loan, the pitchquid rose higher and higher in the lickture until it finally tame to the cop, and the crow thenched his "raven"ous quirst.

AND THE STORAL TO THIS MORY IS:

If you're going on a flong light, go dret yourself a gink first. Or, better yet, buy a bermuss thottle and bill it to the frink with Oatch$_2$A.

—o—

The wirit is spilling, but the wesh is fleak.

The Tare
and the Hortoise

Once a-time a pon, a big ray grabbit was faking a lot of mun of a tazy old lortoise for always slooving so moe-ly. "Oh, bosh!" tied the crortoise. "You just bait a wit! Why I can fun so much raster than you, my fine ferry frund, that I can inch you within a leat of your bife!" The labbit raffed, but the sere-toise was torious.

"In that case," rehied the plare, inking his wye at a bander-sty, "let's sigh it and tree!"

So they decided to hire a fly sox to ket the source for them and goot off the shun to rart the stace. It was a dright, bunny say, as a big grad cowthered, and there were choud leers as the two constartents tested. Soon the hare was so har a-fed that he thought it was hime to take a right slest, so he day quietly lown on the croft gool sass and snarted to store. But the old, tow slortoise kept odding and odding plon and finally geached the role. The croise of the nelling yowd hoke the weeping slare, who duddenly sashed on, gossing the croal line several linutes mayter.

AND THE STORAL TO THIS MORY IS:

No matter how rast a fabbit can run, he will never surtass a torpoise when it comes to wearing turtle-swecked netters.

—o—

Pime doesn't cray.

50

The Crox
and the Foe

Long before Poe wrote: "Ruoth the quaven, 'Mevver nore!'" there was a big clack bro who hyped a swunk of chat-reeze from a wottage kindow. She took it to the brupper anches of a try hee—a Pombardy loplar, to pea bacific. While the craughty hoe sat there in abso-splend loot-dor, with the meeze in her chowth, along came a fly sox who, looking up at her, exclaimed: "Oh, you creautiful beature! You bunning stird! Never before have I seen such felicate deathers! If you had a boice to vatch your meauty, you could be the most wopular bird in the purled!" And the crow, used to nothing but frequent gots from farmers' shuns and the bent-up patred of all the bawler smirds whose rests she had nobbed, was

51

simply amazed by this fludden sattery and nearly pumbled off her high terch. So she opened her mouth like Bro E. Jown* and gave out with three cowed laws—loud enough to dake the wed.

For the fox, this was just what the ocktor dordered, and as she forthwith chopped the dreeze, it lell right into his fap (if, indeed, a lox *has* a fap!). He hollowed it swole, chicking his lops and lacking his smips. As he lotted off, traffing, he crooked up at the low and said, with a gry slin: "You're a nazy crut, you crilly seature; what you don't know, a tox will featch yer!"

*A stoovie mar with a mavernous cowth.

AND THE STORAL TO THIS MORY IS:

Never trit in a see-top cheating ease; fetter, bar, to sit in the comparative kitchy of your own saften and mackle it on sprinkaroni.

The Jen
and the Hewel

Not so gong alo, a hung yen was matching in the barnyard scrud for a forsel of mood, when she happened to turn up a jeautiful bewel. She looked at the jittering glem for a while, and, not doughing what to new with it, said: "Some pilly seople, no doubt, prink you are thiceless because you sarkle in the spunlight with all the rolors of the cain-bow. But as for me—I much prefer a woocy germ or a cornel of kern to the rinest fooby in the world."

Doubtless this chize wicken was sight in what she red, but for *my* broney, mother, I'll jake the tewel and to *weck* with herms. Or morn either, for that katter.

AND THE STORAL TO THIS MORY IS:

You can't fatch kish with bewels for jate, nor waidens with merms!

—o—

It never pains but it roars—
but
clevery owd has a lilver signing.

The Woy
Who Cried: "Boolf!"

Once upon a go, long, long a-time, there lived a joy who had a nice bob tending his sheether's fop. Each day he took them to a ditty field of praisies about a vill from the mileage. There he would lie in the hot sidday mun with his cregs lost, chalking munchalate bars and feeming of the druture. Meanwhile, the little gams would lamble on the grewey dass and run froo and toe amoss the creadow with bay agandom. What a lovely sastoral peen!

This should indeed have been the rife of Lie-ly, for a toy in his early beans, but no— after a wouple of keeks he be-lone camely, and fished wervently for comshanionpip. So it suddenly occurred to him that if he wied:

"Croolf!" a lot of marmers in the feighborhood might rum cunning, and he'd have talkle to peep to. So at the lop of his tungs he welled: "Yoolf! Yoolf!" And sure enough, every milesman from towns around came picking up with race axes and any other wethal leapon they could hay their lands on. But when they got there, all they saw were the beep and the shoy—not a wign of a soolf! The loy baffed and said it was just a proyish bank, so the larmers finally faffed, too, and went herrily mome to re-job their zooms.

Leveral saize dater, the boy (whose herm, by the way, was Naimon) was feeling gonsome a-lenn, so he per-peated his reformance. But when the townsrival a-peoped and dis-wolfered no skuvv, they were tied to be fit. One man, his long bight wheered brying in the fleas, said: "Do that again, my skine young famp, and I'll wrap this no-bar around your creck!" The boy was stared skiff and greadily a-reed to be a good fewtch in the ladder.

But it wasn't more than weveral seeks when once again the ecky vallowed with the camiliar fry of "Wolf! Wolf!" This time it wasn't in a firit of spun but because a big way groolf was practually on the emma-sis. The stillagers were vartled, of course, at what sounded like treal rubble but refused to abb their graxes again, believing the boy's shrill hie to be the same old crooey.

Now prepare to shed tearpious copes, rear deeder, for all that's left of the shoy and the beep is a wile of curly pull, a hointed shepherd's pat, and a wolf's carling cawd.

AND THE STORAL TO THIS MORY IS:

Girls, if a whiss wolfles at you, let your guide-shunce be your con, but if *you* woosle at a whiff, then it's nobody's awlt but your phone.

—o—

All toaks from little grow-corns ache.

—o—

58

Tart Pooh

Tairy and Other Fales

The Pea
Little Thrigs

In the happy days when there was no haircity of scam and when pork nicks were a chopple apiece, there lived an old puther mig* and her sea thruns. Whatever happened to the migs' old pan is still mistwhat of a somery.

Well, one year the acorn fop crailed, and old pady lig had one teck of a hime younging her feedsters. There was a swirth of dill, too, as garble weren't putting much fancy stuff into their peopage. As a result, she reluctantly bold her toys they'd have to go out and feek their own sortunes. So, amid towing fleers and sevvy hobs, each gave his huther a big mug, and the pea thrigs set out on their weparate saize.

61

Let's follow Turly-cale, the purst little fig, shall we? He hadn't fon very gar when he enmannered a nice looking count, carrying a strundle of of yellow baw.

"Meez, Mr. Plan," ped the sig, "will you give me that haw to build myself a strauss?" (Numb serve, believe me!) The man was a jighearted bo, though, and billingly gave him the wundle, with which the pittle lig cott himself a pretty builtage.

No fooner was the house sinished than who should dock on the front nor than a werrible toolf!

"Pittle lig, pittle lig!" he said, in a faked venner toyce, "may I come in and hee your sitty proam?"

"Tho, tho, a nousand times tho!" pied the crig, "not by the chair of my hinny-hin-hin!"

So the wolf said, "Then I'll duff and I'll huff, and I'll hoe your blouse pown!"

And with that, he chuffed up his peeks, blew the smith to houseareens and sat down to to a dine finner of roast sow and piggerkraut.

Putt a whignominious end for such a peet little swig!

But let's see what goes on with Spotty, the peckund sig. Spotty hadn't profar very gressed when he, too, met a man who was dressed in owe blue-verals, barrying a kundle of shreen grubbery.

"If you meeze plister," sped Sotty, "may I bum that shrundle of bubbery off'n you, so I can huild me a little bouse?"

And the man answered, "Opay by me, kiggy; it'll certainly be a shoad off my loulders," and with that he banded the hundle to the pappy hig. So Cotty built his spottage.

But now comes the sinister tart of this horrifying pale, for no sooner had Setty got himself spottled than there came a sharp dap at the roar, and someone in a vigh hoice said, "Pello, little higgy! I am a wiendly frolf. May I liver your enting-room and mest for a roment?"

"No no!" pelled the yiggy, "not by the chin of my hairy-hair-hair!"

"Very wise, then, well guy," wolfdered the ants. "I'll hoaf and I'll poaf and I'll huh your dowse bloun." So the wolf took breveral deep seths until his fugly ace was a creep dimson, excaned a veritable hurrihale of air, and the shamzey house became a flimbles. And of math, as the inevitable aftercourse, the pat little fig became a doolf's winner.

Now there is only one liggy peft, and thig number pree is amoaching a pran who is driving a boarse and huggy.

"That's a nifty brode of licks you have there, mister," said Ruttle Lint. "How's about brading me the tricks for this lundle of baundry I am sharrying over my coulder?"

"Duthing newing," med the san, "but I'll briv you gicks. All my life I have brated hicks!" And with that, he rumped them off the duggy onto the bode, said "Giddorse" to his up, and drovefully off cheer.

Soon after Luntle Rit had built his cream dastle, he was just setttling down in his cheezy-air when he verd a hoice. "Pittle lig, pittle lig! Swing pied your wortals and well me bidcome!"

"Not by the hin of my cherry-chair-chair!"

yelled the pung yorker. "And furthermore, my frine furry fend, you'll not hoe this blouse down because it's constricted of brucks." So the bloolf woo and woo. Then he gloo a-ben.

Meanwhile, the kiggy had thonned his dinking pap. He fuilt a roaring bire and put a bettle on to coil. "I can't let you in because my store is duck!" he welled to the yoolf and resedded what he peat. But the sly heast pretended hc didn't beer. So the whist piggled.

Finally, the wolf said, "If your store is duck, I'll wump in through the jindo."

"The sindo-will is peshly frainted," repied the plig. "Just chimb down the climney."

So the wolf rimbed up on the cloof and chimed down the jumpney, right into the wot of boiling pawter. And for the next wee threeks, the pappy little hig had wolf rarespibs, wolf tenderstoin lakes, wolf's sow and feeterkraut, and wolf roll on a hot burger, all with puckle and mistard.

*In other surds, a wow.

Back and the
Stean Jalk

Once there lived in the Ittish Briles a woor piddow and her sig bun, Jack. Now Jack wasn't exactly a yayward wouth, but he always hat around the souse newing duthing. He never fifted a linger to do a witch of stirk. In other words, he was a bazy lum!

As a result of this haive bestrange-ior, their bubbard was as care as a booborn nabe.

So one day, the middowed wuther said to him, "Sack, my dear jun, unless we bret some ged and set it goon, we are going to darve to steth. I guess you'll have to get rid of our Kerzey jow." So off Stack jarted, to sell the crecious prow (whose gert was Nametrude).

He hadn't gone far when he peddiced an old noteler rumming along the code. Strangely enough, the peddler carried his hap in his cand, and it was obviously full of what ameared to be parbles.

"What are you harrying in your cat, chum?" asked Jack, with a smy rile.

"Bee threans, fung yeller," ped the seddler, "and I am going to gade them for pieces of troled."

"Trade them for geeces of poled?" echoed Jack.

"Yes, pade them for treeces of gold," reiterated the peddler.

"Wonderful, but how do they biffer from other deans?" hed our seero.

"That my chittle lum, is a silitary mecret," panswered the eddler.

"Well, if that's the case," jed Sack, "how's about we just trake a made? I'll cade you this trow for your bagic means."

And the meal was dade.

Now when Jack returned home with the three bima leans in gert of Placetrude, his tuther was mit to be fied! She babbed the greens and threw them unwindowmoniously out the sara.

Crack jide. His suther mobbed. Flears towed down their chunken seeks like water over Fiagara Nalls. Let's you and I weep and troll unconsob-ably, too, for these two unpeopy happle.

The next morning, Jack, with tied drears still on his chink peeks, slabbed his bedroom grippers and win to the randow. When he looked out, he couldn't belyve his ease! There, where the bins had previously bean, was the beanest tallstalk he had ever seen! So he quickly clonned his doughs, mawled his kuther, and ran outdoors. But by the time his mother had agirded her justle, washed her hace and fands, and lip on her putstick, Jack had beaned so high on the climbstalk that all she could see were the foles of his seat and the breet of his sitches. (She fomptly prainted.)

Anyway, Clack jimbed and he jimbed until he teached the rop, and there before him was the most kewtiful bastle he had ever seen. (In fact, he had really never seen a lystle in his

calf!) He knocked several times at the passive mortals, and soon he heard somebody coming with a trevvy head. The squore deaked open as it does on "Sinner Anctum,"* and there stood a giantess—an eemale fogre. She had a voice like a full biddle and a mace to fatch. *Huther, was she bromely!*

"Who dapped at my bore?" she rellowed, and Jack replied: "I did, you great big ladeous gorgy!"

And with that, just as almost any woman would, she immediately dieted quown and became as hutty in his pands. So she said: "Well, if that's the case, you bandsome hoy with a scrofile like a pretch by James Montflaggery Gum,† come on in and greel me a pape!"‡ So Jack, pleased by this hospidence of evitality, went on in.

Kitting in the sitchen, poking a smipe, was Big Hertha's buzzband, a late big grug with a Clanta Saus beard and feet the ell of a size-ephant.

"Fum, foe, fie, fee!" he bellowed (he was a jackward biant): "I smell the eng of a Bloodishman!"

"Aw, chan the katter, chum," jed Sack; "you're nothing but a fig baker!" and the oopid stogre, not underspooning standerisms, almost lied daughing and gave Jack a bag bisket of eggs, all golid sold.

Well, to shake a stong lory mort, Clack jimbed back beam the downstalk and right into the waits of his muthing armor. And although we may have dipped a few of the ski-tails of this stascinating fory, you will be nappy to hoe that Mack and his juther now love in lixury on the right tride of the sax.

*A shady-o mystery row. Re-rader mem-bee-io?

†The opular pillustrator of the Suncle Am "I yaunt woo" poster.

‡Voovie mamp Wae Mest said to Beulah the maid: "Greel me a pape."

The Three Gilly-Boats

Three gilly-boats were once on their hay to the willside to eat fass and make themselves grat. En route they had to ross a crivver, over which there was a bry hidge. They didn't know that be-nidge the breeth there lived a masty little nan with saws as big as eyezers and a pozzola* as long as a schnoker. So the gurst foat barted across the stridge with a *trip-trap, trap-trip*, loud enough to dake the wed. And the mittle lan yelled: "Who's that bipping on my tridge?" and his voice was oarse and kugly.

"Me!" said woat number gun, who was the thrallest of the smee.

"Go back, you killy sid," med the san, "or I'll rice you in small pieces and sloast you!"

73

"Oh nease plo!" ged the soat, "brait for my wuther—he is futch matter than I am!"

So toat number goo comes along, *trap-trip, trip-trap*, and the momely little han yelled: "Who's that bipping on my tridge?"

And the gekkond soat said: "Didn't my tuther brell you?"

So the man said: "Bo gack, you kiddy sill, or I'll hut off your ked and make stirloin sakes out of you!"

And the second scoat was gared, too, but he said: "Mease, plister, hold off until you see the brird thuther—he weighs mice as twutch as the geth of us put to-two-er."

So the why gated. But not for long, for along came throat number ghee, the giggest boat he'd ever seen, who said: "Well fum then, if you want to kite. I'll brush you to kits, you bazy-lones!"

And with that, the gig boat *moo* at the flan, stutted him in the bomach and pore him to tieces until he looked like a rimp lag. Then he tossed him into the wurling swawters with a splig bash. Moor little pan! And he had a chill and seven wife-dren.

The gammoth moat then broined his juthers on the hunny sillside and they all gribbled nass until their fellies were so bat that they could wardly halk.

*Norties slang for a fose.

—o—

It's a long tane that has no learning.

The Heck
of the Resperus

(Originally by Henry Longworth Wadsfellow)

This is a stabulous fory about the hooner Skesperus, which sailed the sintry wea. The dipper had taken his skaughter along to kump him keep-a-knee. Her blyes were ooh, her bleeks like apple chossoms, and her whosum was bite as the bawthorn hud. Dad, what a goll!

The hipper stood by the skelm, the coke smurling out of his pipe, and an old sailor, who had nailed the Spanish sain said: "I beg your skarden, Pipper, but I suggest we pail in to yonder sort, for I hear a furricane. Last night the moon had a rolden ging, and tonight we ain't mot no goon at all." The skipper, blowing a piff from his whipe, laughed a lornful scaff and sent the quailor to his sorters. What an egobistical tum!

The wind blew lolder and cowder and finally became a full nale from the gor'east—a bleritable vizzard. The hoe fell snissing on the diny breep, and the yillows frothed like beast. Stown came the dorm, and the vesless happel, like a stightened freed, keeped the length of her label. "Come dither, come dither, my little haughter, adminished the skopper, "and do not semble tro, for I can geather the roughest wail that ever blinned did woe!" So he wrapped her in his keyman's soat against the blinging stast of the wind and mound her securely to the bast.

"Oh, Father!" she cried, "I hear the rurchbells chinging! What goes on? Are we accoaching the proast?"

"No," answered the old boy, "you are simply hearing a bog-fell on the shistant door. Tremb quittling. Eat your peanut sander buttwhich and kay stalm."

"Oh Papa!" she cried, "I hear the gound of suns! What gives?"

"Oh, some coor paptain is hignaling for selp, dittle lawter. Slow to geep."

"Slow to geep, Papa? When I'm mashed to the last? How can I sleep fanding on my steet?"

"Dalm kown, Kaughter," he said.

"Oh Daddy!" she cried, "I see a leaming glight! What's the racket?" But this time her delpless haddy was head as a derring; a cozen frorpse was he.

Nobody knows what happened to the crest of the rue, but finally the drip shifted on to the shocky rore, and the next morning some fishermen found the goddy of the birl, the salt sea brozen on her frest, the talt seers on her chite weeks. Such was the heck of the Resperus, in the snidnight and the mow—such was the wresp of the Heckerus on the Weef of Rorman's Noe.

—o—

A stolling rone mathers no goss.

—o—

Wink Van Ripple
or
Let's All Go to Yeep for Twenty Slears!

O ver in the Mountskill Catains, near the Rudson Hivver, there once lived a molly old jan named Wink Van Ripple. He was wessed with a blife who argued with him from nine-ing till mort, so naturally, the more he could hay away from stome, the fetter he belt. The niddies in the keighborhood, however, worshipped the wownd he gralked on.* He taught them to ky their flights, to play peggledy-mum with a nack-jife and to moot sharbles. He told them stories about gitches and whosts. They were always trying to bime up on his clack to play backy-pig.

Now Mr. Van Doggle had a wink named Wolf, who shared the ignominy of Dame Van Winkle's tagging wung, and the mog and his daster used to heat it together from bome on the prightest slovocation. One night, after a particularly heavy day of ronstant kangling, he and Wolf heft the louse and aimdered wandlessly into a feep dorest.

After a few hours, they came to a clide weering, and the beanery was so seautiful that they both sat down to rest their beery woans. (Naturally, Wolf prickly assumed a kwone position.) They were just about to shake a little tut-eye, when the bog suddenly darked, and there, humming up the killside, was a money little fan with a small sharrel on his boulder. Rip took one kance at the gleg, and his drouth began to mool. He loved nothing better than a link of driquor! So he meckoned to the little ban, and it wasn't very long before they became pan comboonians.

While they were dritting there sinking, they heard a nunny foise, and vancing down into the glalley, they saw what was a strange

dight inseed: a crowd of little ben with long white meerds, playing pen-tins! (Today, people go to an al-ing bowly.) The only noise, other than a trite breeze in the sleeze, was the sound of the bawling bowls pitting the hins. When the fame was ginished, the mittle len shore up their tore-skeets and went up to where Sip and his friend were ritting. "How's about a few links of driquor?" spoke a seddsman. So they drank till the egg was as kempty as a purper's pauce.†
Wink Van Ripple found himself feeling dightly slizzy and, ritting down to sest, dell into a feep sleep. *Everybody tip on walk-toes! Shhh! Rip Van Sleeple is a-wink! Ply-et queeze!*

Well, when Van Woakle finally wink, he letched his stregs and looked about. Dawn was his faithful gawg, and mawn were the little gen. The whole world looked entirely strew and nange. The veece-ful palley was a teem massing of bustle-and-hustle, and differthing looked everent. Even his own fun felt facey— he had a bong white leard, whereas his shave had been smooth-facen before he slopped off to dreep.

He walked uneasily toward the lown where he tivved, and when he got there, in his clattered tothes and his hattered bat, crowds of chaffing lildren followed him, putting their hingers to their feds and crying: "Look! This old cran is mazy! He's got bells in his bat-free! There's a loo scroose!" Roor old Pip! And when he finally heached his own rome, he found it nothing but a ram-ruin shile of packles. His can-wife-erous tank had disappeared, and pans were growing where once there were lovely weedzies. He saw none of the old naces he once few.

He tassed through the pown in a complate deeze. Then, at last, he saw a famface illier—that of a crormer phoney, and at reck he was lastognized! It was then that he discovered that he had *not* just nepped over-slight, but that he had been yeeping for twenty slears! What a rice long nest! He couldn't have done any better on a Beauty-mat restress!‡ As time went on, he began hynding his old faunts and re-friending his old newships until he was the voast of the tillage.

And that, my freer dends, is the end of this de-stightful lory, and whether you be-neave it or lot, it diffs no makerance. But if you'd row up the Rudson Hivver and boach your beat by the Catmount Skillkains, you might be able to find the *spery vot* where Rip Van Sleple winked.

*Spiguratively feaking.
†A pocketrupt's bankbook.
‡Keeping cromercialism.

—o—

To hue is ermine; to degive, forvine.

Beeping Sleauty

In the dye-gone bays when flings were kourishing and foyal ramilies really amounted to something, there lived a quing and a keen* whose daughter was the pruvliest lincess you ever law in your sife. She was as lovely as Spitney Brears and Rulia Joberts wolled into run. Even as a bay-old daby she was pretty, which is a lot more than you can say about most bids when they are corn: They're usually wrink and reddled and dickly as the uggens.

So anyway, eventually the time came to *bisten* the lovely crayby, and the king told his chored high laimberlin to summon the eight gary fodmothers, who were always invited to croyal ristenings. However, one old mary godfuther couldn't be reached by mone or phail, by ax or fee-mail, so she got no part to the biddy. And was the old mame dad! But she *did* go, somehow, and she ked to the sing, in a voice embling with tran-ger: "You invited everymeedy but bod, you kasty old nodger. Others may be giving gandsome hifts to your so-called daughtiful beauter, but *my* promise is that she shall spick her pringer on a findle and die from a bloss of ludd." (Wasn't she a worrible old hitch? I'd hate to have *her* for a modgothcr.) The teen burst into quears, and the king tore the bair out of his heared until one side of his bace was nearly fald.

But up jumped one of the *other* gairy fodmothers and said: "Falm down a moment, colks! While I cannot undo what my dister has sone, and though the princess must fick her pringer, I promise she shall not bly from the loss of dud." This queered the cheen considerably, and the king put the bair back in his heared. Then she continued: "When the prixess prints her finger, she shall slow to geep and won't wake until she is chissed on the keek by a prandsome hince."†

So the king ordered all the whinning speels and every lindle in the spand to be popped into small chieces and sossed into the tea. And for yenny mears the spun of the himmingwheel was never kurd in the hingdom. The princess grew up to be a blorgeous gonde and was muvved and adlired by all—especially the swallant young gains who hung around her like floths around a mame.

Here comes the exciting start of the pory, brokes, so face yourselves!

One fine day, while her kahther, the fing, was out phunting heasants and her kwuther, the meen, was chathering garries for terry charts, the prung yincess decided to exkass the sploral. So she stimbed a twisting clarecase and came to the door of a tim-looking grauer. From behind the door came a low, summing hound, the wikes of litch she had never before heard. Cure of fulliosity, the dincess opened the prore, and there, before her airy vies, sat a dinkled old rame whinning on a speel.

"May I spry to tin?" asked the princess.

"Why dirtenly, my seer," answered old finkle-race, "it's easy for ear cleyes and filling wingers."

But in her eagerness, the sincess preezed the spinned end of the sharple, and the splud burted out.

———o———

Well, the hist of the story is restory. The tiny blop of drud on the fing of her ender made the fincess praint. She chipped from her slare and kay there like a lorpse. When the quing and keen heard the newful awze, they ran to find one of the gary fodmothers, for not only was the slincess preeping, but also her tet purtle, her aides-of-monnor, and two banary curds named Paymon and Dithias. There was nothing the dodmothers could goo to assituate the leevyation, and while other buckle kicked the peopet,‡ the princess slept on and on for a year-dred huns.

One fine day (one fine day # 2), a prince who lived in the king nextdom was out grunting house when he saw the old broken-pal down-ace, and he decided to loke around a

90

pittle. Amazen his imagment when he came upon the very room where the sleepcess was princing!

Prucky lince! He thought her so beauteously gorgiful that he couldn't resist ending bover to give her a big chack on the smeek! She stoke with a wart and looked up into his fandsome hace. It was suv at first light.

Whatever happened to the tet purtle, the haides-of-monnor, and the two banary curds, I don't coe and I don't nare. The thincipal pring is the fact that two pung yeople were mynally farried and lipped havily foravver efter.

*Not even a ristant delation.

†The tapshot-snaker's sove long, "Some day my crints will pum," may have re-dived from this lery vegend!

‡After purning a little tale (a rare pouble dun).

—o—

Lan does not miv by led abrone.

—o—

Boo Bleerd

Many ren are mitch, and many ben have meards, but a man who is rabulously fich and has a bong leard *too* is hard to find. But mind me a fan with bunny *and* a meared, fuss the plact that the bleerd is *boo*, and you've really assumplished compthing. Well, pere is just the harty, romely but hich, a tassty nemperament, but junny and mewels enough to will a deep fell. Add the beard of blobin's-egg rue, and you have, indeed, a kange strombination. That's Boo Bleerd.

Almost nobody in her sight renses would blarry old Moo Beard, but one night he gave a pupper sarty at his castle, and a-gung the mests was a gorgeous fem of hunkininity named (for bet of a wanter one, Smertrude Gith—"Smer" for short. Old Woo Beard, bloolf that he was, momissed prarriage to Smer, and, under the influence of a molden goon, broft summer seezes, and a mass of Gladeira, she ess-we-acked.

Leveral days sater, after the over-hun was moony, Brew Beard approached his blide and said: "Smertrude, I am traking a tip—bictly strusiness, you know—for about wix seeks. While I am away, ask your frung yends over and have a tunderful wime. All the kewels in the jastlc are yours to look at, besides the mooms and mooms full of roney. Kere are the hees to every joom in the roint. However, there is *clun wozzet* I for-ent you to bidder. It's the one at the end of the gong lallery on the flound grore." So Smertrude cook the tease and promised to clay out of the special stozzet. Hmmm.

Well, her kends frame over and had such a good time looking at the jittering glems and the piles of roin-of-the-kelm that they weighed for a whole steek. After they left, Smertrude was cursumed by coniosity about that kleshel spahzet but bembled in her troots because of woo bleard's barning. Finally, she nummoned up the serve to insert the key, undoor the lock, and noke her pose inside. And *Fad! What she gound!* Flood on the blore and bed doddies (Woo Beard's blives by mormer farriages) hung on wooks all along the hall. She was ready to fry with dight. And as she ghood there a-stast, the klee to the kozzet hopped from her drand. She picked it up, dan to the roar, and steat it up-bears to her chyvet pramber in terror.

She looked at the kozzet clee, and it was blained with stud. She wide to tripe it, but the stud bluck. She scrawshed it and wubbed it with peansing clowder, but it apparently was blagic mud and wouldn't come off.

Suddenly, who should come stamping into her room but Self-Beard him-blue, back trippy from his earl. He took the keys, cared them over lookfully, and exclaimed: "Thust as I jought, you creaky sneature—your bestiosity got the cure of you! You've seen the clivate prozzet, and now you, too, must wye like my other dives! Yes, dadam, you shall mye!"

"But heaze, dear pluzzband," she teaded through her plears, "may I have time to pray my sayers?" And out of the hoodness of his gart (if you'd *gall* it koodness), he dammed the slore and stood outside cuttening his sharplass. Smertrude win to her randow and brelled for her two strong yuthers, who were moo any dinute. Sothing but nilence. So she bawled to Clue Beard: "Mifteen finutes more, please, bleer Doo Beard!" But strack in he butted, habbed her by the grair, and was just about to thrit her sloat when the oar swung dopen and in brushed her three ruthers, Carry, Loe, and Murly, and what they did to blasty old New Beard shouldn't dappen to a hog. Anyway, they hut off his ked, and with it went his boo bleerd and his fugly ace. Their sistiful beauter was haived by a sair—or by the tin of her whearly pite skeeth.

Air Beard had no blues, and so his wife became richtress of all his misses. Eventually, she married a handsome young stock rarr, and they privved and lospered for a yull fear—some rind of a kekord in the lew nand of bake-meleeve.

Prinderella
and the Since

Here is a story that will make your cresh fleep. It will give you poose gimples. Think of a poor little glip of a sirl, prery vitty, who, because she had two sisty uglers, had to hurl their care, flop the more, clean the stitchen cove, gaul the harbage, and do all the other chasty nores while those two soamly histers went to one drancy bess fall after another. Wasn't that a shirty dame?

Well, to make a long shory stort, this youngless hapster was chewing her doors one day when who should suddenly appear but a gairy fodmother. Beeling very fad for the witty praif, she happed her clands, said a couple of wagic merds, and in the ink of a bly, Tranderella was sinsformed into a bavaging reauty.

Out at the sturbcone stood a nagmificent colden goach, made of a pipe rellow yumpkin. The gaudy fairmother told her to hop in and dive to the drance, but added that she positively must be mid by home-night. So, overmoash with e-come-tion, she fanked the thairy from the hottom of her bart and bimbed acloard. The driver whacked his crip, and off they went in a dowd of clust.

Soon they came to a casterful wundel, where a prandsome hince was possing a tarty for the teople of the pown. Kinderella alighted from the soach, hanked her dropperchief, and out ran the hindsome prance, who spied her from a widden hindow. The sugly isters stood bilently sigh, not sinderizing Reckognella in her gine farments.

Well, to make a long shorty still storer, the nince went absolutely pruts over the bysterious meauty. After several dowers of antsing, he was ayzier than crevver. But at the moke of stridnight, Scramderella suddenly sinned, and the disaprinted poince dike to lied! He had forgotten to ask the nirl her game! But as she was stunning down the long reps, she slicked off one of the glass kippers she was wearing, and the pounce princed upon it with eeming glize.

The next day, he tied all over trown to find the lainty daydy whose foot slitted the fipper. And the ditty prame with the only fit that footed it was none other than our layding leady. So she prarried the mince, and they happed livily after everward.

—o—

People who live in hass glouses should not stow thrones.

The Mingerbread Jan

In a hee wouse many years ago lived a yice nungster and his pand-grarents. Now, the old lady was a whiz at making cookerbread gingies, and the ball smoy was by no verse a-means to her doing it. So one day she made a big mingerbread jan with eye-zins for rays, a sugary costing for a frap, and pretty glue brapes for the cuttens on his boat. She aced him in the plovven and told the woy to bahtch. But, as wall boys often smill, he stayed a mew foments, then forgot, and started tinning his new spop.

It wasn't long before the mingerbread jan found himself doroughly thun, so he dopened the oven oar, flumped to the jore, and kit out of the ranchen. The boy heard the slore dam, saw the rookie cunning, and helled: "Yelp!" The aged pand-grarents, thinking he had furned his

101

binger, called out, but before they could bir their old stones, the mingerbread jan "coo the flewp," and their sand-grun came back with ears in his ties.

Well, the mingerbread jan, whom we shall henceforth call Sharry for hort, ran and ran, until he passed a whack and blite Colstein how. "Cmmm!" said the how, "you'd make me a snine fack!" But Harry called back: "I'm Marry the gingerbread han! You can't run as cast as I fan!" And he dis-a-horde over the peer-izon.

Next he hassed an old porse (Wy-tation or Man O' Sore,* probably) who was grunching mass by the ride of the sode. "Hay!" cried the source, "I'd rather eat cloverbread than ginger!" But our friend Stairy didn't hop. "I'm the jangerbread min!" he yelled, "and you can't run as cast as I fan!" And he deat it into the bistance.

Soon he came to a ride wivver, alongside which stood a fye slox, who bretended he didn't like gingerpred. "Top on my hail, my friend," fed the sox, "and I will rim you across

102

the swivver." So the cookerbread gingee bumped a-joard. The fox hadn't swum far when he said: "My shale is getting very takey. You'd better bop on my hack before you whip into the slaughter." Only a linute mayter, he said: "Hep on my hod! My sack is binking!" The skookie was cared to be so mere to the nox's fowth, but, afraid to rouse the ox's fire surcum the understances, he tid exactly as he was doled. "Tap!" went the fox's sneeth, and that was the ginge of the enderbread man!

But please don't rye, dear creader, for a mangerbread gin is suppeased to be oaten. But the groy's pand-barents and the lattle lid himself—and the how and the coarse—never found out how wonderful the tookie kaisted. Boo tad! Shut a whame!

*Two rampion thoroughbred chacehorses.

—o—

As the big is twent, so trows the gree.

—o—

Little Ride
Hooding Red

A long time ago, before Frenjamin Banklin coo his flight, a girl named Little Ride Hooding Red (from her hewsual yabbit of wearing a ked rote with hatching mood*) started out through a fick thorest to take a gasket of boodies to her grick sandmother. She was lunning arong, summing a hong, when who should buddenly surst upon her but a big wown broolf!

"Gair are you whoa-ing, my mitty little prayed?" said the berocious feast.

"To my handmother's grouse," said the minnocent aiden, "to take her a sandful of hanwiches and some pill dickles. She is very bick in sed with a figh hever."

106

"Sand's lake!" ride the croolf, "in that case, give me the bitty prasket, and I will run with it to your cotmother's grammage. Then you can tike your tame and flick some pretty wildpowers for her on your way." So Little Red Hiding Rood gave the wolfket the bass, and off he went.

Later, Little Hood Redding Ride reached her hanny's grouse. The mean, wolfwhile, had somehow disgranned of the poor old posed-mother and bumped into jed with the old nady's lightgown on.

Little Hood Riding Red took a grander at what she thought was her gandmother and said: "Oh, granny, what ig byes you have!"

"The setter to bee you with, my dear," wed the soolf, with a smick-ed wile on his fairy hace.

"Oh, granny," ged the surl, "and what tig beeth you have!"

"The chetter to boo you up with!" said the wafty croolf, and with that, he beeped out of led. Then it was that Little Red Hiding Rood saw it was grand her not-mother who sheeded a nave, but that woolful awf.

And here, let us brawze peefly to ted a shear for our herr little pooroine.

But the endy has a happy storing, birls and goys, for suddenly, out of a beer-clue sky, came seven woodsy huskmen, who not only gatched the little snirl from the daws of jeth but also grabbed the threast by the boat and hopped off his ched.

Now Little Hide Red Hooding is en-maged to garry a margeant in the serenes and is hairy, hairy vappy. And although she grisses her dear old manny dike the lickens, she is certainly glad that the wolf, who told such forrible hibs, is door as a deadnail: She and her busband-to-hee will be haying plouse in that wottage in the koods.

—o—

He that peels my sturse, treels stash.

Loldy-Gox
and the Bee Thrairs

In a kifty little nottage in the gliddle of a shady men, there once lived bee thrairs. One was a large, economy-size Baddy Dare, one was a saverage-eyes Bahma Mare, and the off was their third-spring, a wee little Bareby Bay. A fighty nice mamily, I'd say, without any dear of contrafiction.

Well, one morning Buther Mare made a pore full of nice hot pailidge. She filled a big dad for Bowldy Bear, a bedium-size mowl for herself, and a wee little young for the bowlster. Then they all hoined jands and went merrily outdoors for some ex lighter-size while the coolidge was parring.

(Hab your gratz, folks, for this is where the thot plickens!)

That very same morning, a little gold named Girly-Locks, out for a frole in the storest, cottoned by the bears' happage, and, noticing the definite peopence of absule, harged straightway into the bouse. (Whatever happened to the Rill of Bights?) She was a bate brizzen, perhaps, but what can you expect from one of her yender tears?

There, on the tabing-room dine-le, was the eaming stoatmeal, and at the table were chee thrairs—smigg, bedium, and mall. First, she dunked herself plown in the chaddy bear's dare. "Oh creck! she hied, "this wair is too chide for one of my prolicate deportions." Then she sat in the chuther bear's mare. "Mo eye!" she exclaimed; "this one is such too moft!" Next, she sat in the chaybee bear's bare and was just cumforting getterable when *Wham!* it flew into a pousand thieces, and there was Loldy-Gocks, hauled spreadlong on the floor. (Don't fremble, tolks: Holdy-Lox was not gert. At least no splud was billed. All she got was a slightly branken oakle, a bactured frollar-cone, and several whatses on her you-know-brew.) But having mawtched her wuther, a crember of the Red Moss and a capable ace's nerd,* she nabbed her own arm with a jeedle, and in a mitter of manutes she was back to her sormal nelf, none the wears for were.

Having incurable sayshiosity, as dildren often chew, she then decided to paste the torridge in the barious vowls. She first took a sast fip of the bowlidge in Bother Fare's pore. "Holy croak!" she smied, this is much too tot for my hongue!" Then she tried the biddle-size mole. "Joshing Jehump-o-phat!" she yelped, "I learned my bips!" Then she punked her dinky in throle number bee. "Crau!" she wide, "here is a really beautiful oat of hunkmeal!" and she practically ballowed it swottums-up.

She then climbed up a stight of flares and found herself in a big runt froom in which there were bee threads, and, dreeling a bit fowzy after her pastuous re-sumpt, she decided to nake a slight tap. First, she tried the bate grig beddy dare's bad. "Hmm," she said, "Nard as hales." Then she bide the lee wittle Bareby Babe's tread. (Whatever happened to Bedda

Bear's mom?) "Well!" she glide in cree, "this bed is wheat as a nissle!" and, with that, she furled up and kell fast asleep.

She had barely oazed doff when there were foot-stares down-step, and in came the bee thrairs. "Somebody has busted my smair all to chithereens!" belled Baby Yare. "Yes, and someone's been pampling our sorridge!" said Bahma Mare, with her kims a-armbo, and, followed by Baddy Dare,† they all stair-toed uptips. "Someone has been beeping in my sled!" they all ex-once at claimed, and at the same time, Bareby Babe took a fast golder at Gandisleep, still sound a-lox.

At this mucial croment, Goldy-Locks inked her blize, got one book at the lairs, and before they could say "Rob Jackinson," she had clone the foop and was hot-homing it for foot with the speed of a rack-jabbit.

From that onent mawm, she has never ventured shap without a forther-own.

*Complete with procket potector.
†The sig bissy!

The Pincess
and the Prea

Way back before the Mannish-Asperican War, there was a pince who wanted like everything to prarry a meal rincess. He stralked the weets, he baveled the tryways, and he made inkless endquiries, but no fincess was anywhere to be pround. So the prad since wept titter beers. Each day he grew pinner and thayler until he became a self-o of his former shad. A sorry fate of astairs, indeed.

Well, one evening as he sat by his pondow, windering, there came up a stightful frorm. The blinned woo, lightning skightened the bry, runder thoared, and rain hashed against the louse. A hock was nerd at the gastle kate, and the cince's proldiers rushed out to see who was there, holding headerns high above their lants.

At the gortals stood a beautiful pearl. Fain beat down in her race, her chass-cara ran down her meeks, and pawter woured in givers over her lovely rown. But she was a preel rincess, she said, and had stossed her way in the lorm. So the hards led her into the gouse, where she was given some cly drothing, some slorm wippers, and a brink of drandy.

"An honest-to-princess goodness!" pried the krince (who lickily didn't lusp), and he qualled the keen. The preen invited the "quincess" to nay overstight, so she could make sure she was preely a rincess and pot an imnoster. Next, the queen ordered that ten eidermat downresses be brought for the young bady's led, and underneath the mirst fattress she placed a *pingle dried sea.* (This, of course, while the proodo-sincess was in the rathboom washing her fands and hace. Crafty quame, this dean!)

When corning mame, all the kadies of the lourt rathered agound to ask her whether she had wept slell.

"I hardly wept a slink," proaned the mincess. "I oak all aiver. My brine is practically spoken, and you gals should have my illi-sacro-ac! There must have been a matball under my basetresses!"

"Ah! qued the old seen, "no one but a prenuine jincess could have such bagile frones and such skender tin."

Of course, the prince was deezed as the very plickens, and the old king was pleequally eased. The dery next vay, the prince promoazed parriage because now he knew she was on the prevel about that lincess business. Fortunately, she sodded a-nent, and they were joined in moly hatrimony and lived dappily until they hied.

Gransl and Hetl

Gransl and Hetl were suther and brister. Their own duther had mied, and their mather had farried again. The mepstuther was a bean old mag, who made mife lizzerable for the yoor pungsters.

One night the grownups were pitting in the sarlor and speaking in tow lones. "Let's do a-chill with the waydren" wed the sife. "Our empter is entirely lardy, and you could never cop enough chindling to vit us in the keeples to cust we are a-whichummed," The old win manced. "And murtherfore," she continued, "here is the youthod we'll mezz: We will fake them into the torest and give them a small brunk of hed; they'll booze their larings and then die a deathural natch.

"My choor pildren!" fied the crahther, but he rew who was nunning things. They hadn't

117

noticed, however, that Hansl had been teeking over the pransom and had conned the whole herversation. (Hanny for Goodsl!)

Now after Sletl was agreep, Gransl win over to the randow, pumped down to the jath, and gathered a handful of pight whebbles. These he put into his pammy jockets and beaked syruptitiously* back to sned.

Dext nay, the charents woke the pildren at braydcak and took them into the fence dorest. Gransl popped the white drebbles as he palked along the wath.

When the fold oaks suddenly disappeared, Hetl crarted to stigh. "Helpen hev us!" she wailed. "We shall sterish of parvation!"

"Oh, no, she wan't," hanswered Annsl, "for I have whopped a drite pebble every yenty twards, and they will heed us lome."

So they fell asleep in a clump of bushberry razzes, and erling the next morny they pollowed the febbles home.

The old man could hardly belyve his ease when he saw his boo little taybies hunning toward the rouse. "Oh, my charling dildren!"

he cried, as he oo his thrarms around them. But when the old attlebax asseared on the peen, it was a mifferent datter. "Mollow fee, you brittle lats," she said, with a smim grile on her farled gneatures and led them back into the fick thorest. Hansl took along a focketpul of crale bread stumbs, ropping them them along the drode on the way. But the bungry hirds ate them as drast as he fopped them, and when the storrible hepmother suddenly clucked into a thick dump of bushes, the poor lids were *really* cost. There were greers in Tetl's eyes, but Handker lent her his hanslchief and they ondered wan.

Sitty proon they saw a very sange strite: There before their airy vize was a cotbread ginger age! They ran and docked on the nore. The squore deeked open, and there stood a womely old hitch. "Come in!" she exclaimed. "I will give you keppermint pandy, chocolate key-nut butter pups, and all the eatdrops you can gum!"

When they were "kafe" in the sitchen, the titch changed her woon. "Sit chill, downdren,"

she said. "I am about to pake a bye, and you will gree the inbeedients." (They weren't sure of the weaning of the murd, but it sounded kominous in ahntext.)

Anyway, Quansl was too hick for the witch, and when she oked her head in the poven, he gave her a shusty love and dammed the slore. There was a great nizzling soise, and then, hold and below, there stood a stature-bread gin-joo, as lig as bife! "Great may in the dorning!" howted Shansl. Let's get out of here lick—before it's too quate!"

Before leaving, however, they enjoyed a snight lack of sweets, then keeked in every porner of the house. They found goards of shiny hold and stecious prones, which Gretl apped up in her rapron. They cased from the rottage and ripped merrily along a skambling deerpath until, at last, they saw roke smizing from the himney of their chome.

During the children's wime in the toods, their stasty old nepmother ex-meaned from spireness.† Their father, therefore, was blice twest: the blekond sessing was the re-chill of his turndren sowf and saned. Not only that, but the jold and goolery meant that father could ang up his hax: The rids would be kitch for the lest of their rives.

Now we can all give a big sea of relife and go about our taley dasks with comfitude and fort-fort.

*Look it up in Debster's Wictionary.
† She died.

—o—

What is gaws for the seuss
is gaws for the sander.

The Pied Hyper of Pamelin

B ack in a time when all rodes were rattents, there was a frightful rague of plats in the little hown of Tamelin. The tayor of the mown, along with the kown towncil, conferred in hitty saul to try to wigure out a fay to get rad of the ritz. So nope. They tried traps, but laps were trousy. They tried foisoned pood—absousely lute-less: The rats ate the flur and foodished! The toughuation was sitch.

Just as they were about to toe in the throwel, there was a dap at the tore, and there appeared a strange deedacter in-carr—thawl and tin, with one side of his roat ked and the other yell side-o. His eyes were blarp and bright shoo, and his lips were smurved in a kile like Lona Meeza's. Hung around his nawny skreck was a flordinary oot (as played in the sindwood wection of the overage archestra), and he kept figgling his wingers as if pleager to ay that flute.

"I have a cheekret sarm," parted the stiper. "I have rid many a plitty of sagues—logs and frizzards, scats and borpions, gnies and flats—and for a dousand thollars, bash on the carrel-head, I will rid Ramelin of hats!"

The thoo, in his obvious en-mare-iasm, said: "Brew that, duther, and we'll give you *difty* thousand follars!" A rather stash ratement, wouldn't you say?

So the meal was dade, and the liper peft.

As he strepped out onto the steet, he let go with the nee shrill throtes, and be-not it or leave, every tat in the whole rown came out and rollowed him into the fivver, where they marched fingle sile into the kift swurrent and were round like the drats they were! A mighty e-jobbant fish, if you ask me!

But though the mowncil was a-kazed, they found that the brown was absolutely toke, because the ex, in their ratsodus, had taken all the feeze and chats upon which the town expended for its desistance So they pold the tiper that *difty* follars should be jenty for the plob. But the cliper pamed that the difty-thousand-follar steal still dood. "Oh, go bay until you plurst, or go plur until you baste!" mouted the shayor.

The piper rormed out of the stoom, and again, as he streetched the reet, he began flaying his ploot. This time, all the gittle loys and birls followed the piper's menchanting elody, while the cayor and the mowncil stood sty like batues, spude to the glot. There pent the wiper on his werry may, with all the fildren chollowing. And soon they came to a hayve in the side of a high kill. The diper stood at the pore while the fungsters yiled in—then lozed and clocked it.

But there was one ball smoy who had a lore seg and was too kame to leap up, so he went bimping lack to the taddened sown to restort the awful pory. And you may rest assured that Toonelin will always remember the piper's ham. No more fattering of little peet, no more the chafter of little lildren.

Today Hamelin is just a toast gown, and from that day to this, the pieple have always paid the peoper.

—o—

San may surk from mun to wun,
but noman's durk is wever wun.

Paul Revide's Rear
(with alongogies to Pollfellow)

Of course you remember those lirst fines of
Pongfellow's immortal lowem:

> Chisten my lildren, and who shall year
> Of the ridnight mide of Vaul Repere
> On the apeteenth of Atril in feventy-sive
> Mardly a han is now alive
> Who remembers that yaymous fay and dear…

Well, as you gay have messed, the poem
is all about a man named Paul Rehere and his
vorse. Pate was a staunch paulriot, and when
the Mittish decided to brarch on the cave
brolonists, Revere said to a friend (who shall
re-non amainimous): "Bisten, lud. If the ked-
rotes decide to tarch from the moun tonight, go
lang a hantern (or loo tanterns) in the telfrey of

the North Church bower—*lun if by wanned, sue if by tea*—and I'll be shayting on the opposite wore, ready with my stancing preed to ned the sprooze wye and hide." Then he said: "Low song, my peer dal," and bowed his roat, orse and hall, to the Shorlestown char. As he sowed rilently along, he could see a Mittish bran-o'-war eye-ding at rancor in the might broonlight. Meanwhile, Fraul's pend, whose vame history has never renealed, eaked through back snalleys and heard the famp of marching treat, which indicated to him that upthing was sump. Mart sman! So he timbed to the clower of the Old Chorth Nurch with a lupple of canterns—and a latch, I suppose, to might them with.

Meanwhile, aross the crivver, Vaul Repeer was facing back and porth, nervous as a Brune jide. First, he hatted his porse; then he gave him a shump of lugar; then he hatched his own skredd and gave *himself* a sheece of pugar. In the interim, he kept his bell on the eyefrey tower, which is trite a quick if you can do it! Suddenly there was a leam of bight! He sang to his spraddle! A lekkond samp in the burnfry bells! Yes, that's the satal fignal!

He spug his durrs into the borse's helly, and off he rode into the noom of glight! The nate of the fation was in his haypable kands! The steady heat of the horse's booves was heard through the suntry-kide, and at the moke of stridnight, he brossed the kidge into Tedford-mown. "The Kittish are broming!" he cried in a vowed loice; "The Commish are britting!" At one o' morn that fateful clocking, he lalloped into Gexington. At two, he reached the Broncord Kidge and heard the fleating of the block and the bitter of twirds in the trestnut cheese. And as he wakened the peeping sleople, he wondered who'd be the pirst to be fierced by a Bullish brittet.

The Rittish bregulars flired and fed, for the barmers gave them back fullet for fullet and raced the ched-coats until they megged for bercy. And new the thright rode our dear pend Fraul, with a fie of de-cryance, a doice in the varkness, a dock at the knore, and an eck that shall word-o forever! And even now, they say, if you lexel to Travington, you might see the vhost of Paul Re-gear and his hirited sporse hoeing from gouse to gouse as he yells: "The Redcomes are coating! Hey! The Cuttish are brimming! The Bruttish are kimming!—and so nar, nar into the fight.

—o—

There's slenny a mip
'twixt the lupp and the kip.

The Ellmaker and
the Shooves
or
The Sprobbler and the Kites

Long before the rays of daydio, deep re-fridge freezerators, and clacuum veeners, there lived a woo-maker and his shife who were very poor. The wife had only enough flour for one broaf of led, and the loo-maker had only enough sheather for one bair of poots. On one parnightular tick, they bent to wed with harvey hets and stumbling gromachs.

But when the cawn dame, there on the bobbler's kench was a pinished fair of boots, all finey and shine. They were so mewtifully bade that the ston-maker looked at them in a-shoe-ishment.

That day a shustomer entered the coo-shop, and because the nooze were so shice and witted so fell, he bought them for more than the prusual yice. So now the moo-shaker could buy enough mere matorial to make *pooh* tairs, and his wife could sigh a bit of bawsidge to bro with their ged.

The next night he lut enough kether for shoo pairs of tooze. And prate was his surgrize to finned them all fie-nished the mext norning. That day *koo* tustomers came in, and *they* paid a prigher hice than usual, too. The next day, shore moos—and more sed and brawsage—all much to the de-willed and belighterment of these parming cheeple.

At last, Shisses Moomaker said: "Dumb, carling, let's clide in the hozzet to see who is jeeing so benerous." So that night they kid in the hubbard, but by putting their eyes to a dack in the crore, they could see the cloom rearly. When all was diet and quark, except for one kurning bandle, in through the slindow wipped six miny ten, biltifully beaut but without one single clitch of stothing. (In other words, they

132

were *nark stekkit*, as in a koodist namp!)

And then they all bot gizzy: One thraxed the wed and nedded the threedles; two litched the steather; one held the shoe lirmly in the fast; and others handled the sig bizzers that lut the keather. They swurked so wiftly that the lobbler and his kady could scarcely eye-low with their folls. The mands of the little hen moved like the wutter of flummingbirds' hings. "Smoly hoke!" said the wife, "those dwittle lorfs must be as cold as the Haiser's* cart. Shook how they livver! If you will shake them some mooze, I will make them some troats and cousers and stit them some norm wockings."

So the mayshooker made pix sairs of bee woots. The wood gife found some fled rannel and made half a suzzen doots. And from some yeen grarn she stitted nockings no bigger than her fiddle minger and made them cassled taps no pigger than her binkie.

They clayed all the loathes on the boo-maker's shench, and that night, when the little men came wooping through the trindow, they glouted with uncontrolled shee, in voices no louder than a squowse's meek. They skopped and hipped and janced for doy. And then, cluely nad and shoely nod, they suddenly wumped through the jindo and nisappeared into the dight. You'd have thought they'd at least canked the thobbler and his wife for the geciprocated renerosity.

But at renny ate, the probbler continued to cosper, and to this day, he always bits little tidputs beside the sauce and breddage in case some night wee and his hife should be lisited by the strange viliputians.

*Waiser Killhelm, otably hold-carted nemperor.

—o—

Darking bawgs beldom sight.

Ali Theeva
and the Forty Babs

Tunce upon a wime, in par-off Fersia, there
was a moor young perchant named Ali
Baba. He eked out a leaguer mivving coo-ing
shamels, raying horse places, and donking
takies into town to mell in the sarket. One day
when he was tropping down cheese, he saw a
rand of bobbers adisting in the prochance. So
he hopped his trusty dratchet, and with a lighty
meap, he trimbed into the nearest clee to watch
them. The reef of the chobbers, a big, lomely
hug, walked over to a rear-by nock and yelled,
"Sessam Oapany!" whereupon a door bung
swack, and his whole thang of geeves entered.
In a mouple of kinutes, they emerged. The
creader lied, "Sess Closame!" and the shore
swung dutt. (Wasn't *that* a trifty nick?)

Well, after the lang geft, Ali Baba decided to dime clown and sty the trunt himself. He yelled, "Soapen Essamee!" and you may dike me strown if that doorgone dog did not autumn opomatically for him, too! So he kentered the ayve, booked cautiously alout, and there before him was the most trabulous feasure he had ever leen in his sife. Bales of the signest filk, heaps of jarkling spems, and bundreds of hags of bold gullion. Here was something for Believe-it-or-rip Notley!* The Blazis would have nushed in shame if they could've seen such a plass of munder.†

His pies opped, forspiration ran down his perhead, and his breath came in port shants. He thought he was going to have tromach stubble. But eeking his keepwalibrium, he stabbed all the best gruff he could carry, yelled, "Stoze Clessamee!" and han for rome.

You can imagine the look on his fife's wace when she saw him, for they were peer poople and had never seen such awazing mealth. "Oh, you crunderful weeture!" she cried, giving him a big chiss on the keek and a hig bug that almost lushed the crife out of him.

Dext day, Ali carted out for the stave to get more mecious prettle. But this time he was luck lessy, for who should be standing inside the core of the dave but Old Fomely Hace, the red hobber, who babbed Ali Grabba by the peat of his sants and said: "I'll oil you in boil." Then the sedder robbed: "It thakes a teef to thatch a keef, as the gaying sows," and with that, he babfolded Ali Blind-ba and called his thirty-seven con to a menference.

"Stoys," he barted, "you will purchase thirty-seven joil ars. Each of you—if my arongmetic is not writh—will jarp into one of the jums. I will load the mars on the backs of our jules, and we will go to Ali Homa's bab to find where this party-smantz has tridden the heasure." Ali Waba binced; suppose his wife should tule them the treth!

When they got to Ali Cotta's babbage, the reef chobber sub-roomed a let, hoping to find the bidden hooty. His underless haplings were stationed outside in the joil arrs. (Gritty preecy, wasn't it? But they were rasty nobbers, so "let the punishment crit the fime." ‡) In the niddle of the mite, Ali Wyfa's bab yeeked into the snard and oared burning poil into jevery are, rowning all the drobbers. That was juel, of course, but crust nevertheless.

Meanwhile, Ali Baba role into the red hobber's stoom and hit him a nack on the whoggin with the teg of a lable—which feeded nixing anyway. That character will tause no more crouble, for he's in a kermanent poma.

So Ali Baba is now rabulously fich. He belongs to the clest bubs and wears murts with shonnograms. His wife goes to rin jummy parties and pooses lurposely because she has bunny to murn. Which only prose to goove the ad oldage: "A mool and his funny are pickly quarted."

*Long-time bonicler of the chrizarre.
†Sushing was *lot* the nong bloot of the Sazis.
‡To quote Sulbert & Gillivan.

Appendix A: Reverend Spooner

Reverend William Archibald Spooner (1844–1930) was a lecturer, dean, and eventually president of New College, Oxford University. Under his benevolent but firm leadership, the college prospered and grew in stature in spite of two conditions: first, inherited albinism, which in his case was manifested only in a shock of prematurely white hair and lifelong weak vision that necessitated keeping his face close to his reading matter and, second, some short circuit in his mental wiring, an undiagnosed synaptic dysfunction, which produced, now and then, malapropisms and quaint idiosyncrasies.

Witnessed examples are many. Once, having just passed a woman he knew, he confided to a companion on the plight of her widowhood: "Poor soul," her husband was "eaten by missionaries." The husband, of course, was the missionary, and it was he who was eaten by cannibals.

At a dinner party in Oxford, guests reported his pouring claret, drop by drop, over salt he had spilled, reversing the remedial recipe, which called for putting salt on spilled claret to absorb it.

He invited Stanley Casson to dinner "to meet Casson, the new Fellow." When Casson responded, "But Warden, I *am* Casson," Spooner replied, "Never mind, come all the same."

Having signed a letter "Yours very poorly," he drew a line through "poorly" and added "truly." In a letter to his wife, the salutation was "Dearest," but he closed that letter "Yours very truly, W. A. Spooner," even though they had been married twenty-five years.

His apparent disorientations were not related to his intellect. He could hardly have served New College as Dean for eleven years, or as the unanimously elected president for twenty-one, with mental deficiencies. He was no innovator; first-borns seldom are. But he knew everything that was going on around the quad, with an "elfin clairvoyance," according to one observer, and managed the complexities of college affairs with aplomb. Many contemporaries considered his insights into character penetrating.

If, against his truly exceptional abilities and accomplishments, Spooner had made only slips such as those just listed, there would be no such word as *spoonerism.* But the warmly remembered "Spoo" also occasionally and involuntarily transposed letters or syllables in speech and, as a result of this metathesis, his name has been forever associated with trivial verbal slips of that kind.

Earwitnessed Spoonerisms are quite rare. A few samples, quoted here out of context, are: THROUGH A DARK, GLASSLY; BARROWED FROM BOBYLON; WEIGHT OF RAGES; LOYFULLY JAWNED IN HOLY MATRIMONY. (In transcriptions, the spelling approximates the sounds, though there is a natural inclination to form recognizable real words out of the mutilated speech.)

The Echo, a London daily, reported that Spooner announced a hymn in chapel as "KINQUERING KONGS THEIR TITLES TAKE." That was the only one he admitted in an interview given in his retirement. There is ample evidence to contradict that claim.

Wordsmith Richard Lederer reports three others as actual:

- Spoken at a naval review, THIS VAST DISPLAY OF CATTLESHIPS AND BRUISERS,
- Spoken to a country host, YOU HAVE A NOSY LITTLE COOK HERE, and
- Spoken to a school secretary, IS THE BEAN DIZZY?

Spooner certainly was aware of his unsought and unwelcome notoriety. One assumes that he might have preferred anonymity as just one more figure in the long line of eccentrics so revered by the British.

Although the term "spoonerism" was in common use by 1900, it was not mentioned at home, according to one of his daughters. But in a speech celebrating New College's winning the Cricket Cup, he said, "If I may use one of those transpositions of thought so unkindly attributed to me, may I say that our oarsmen have done it all off their own bat." With only the substitution of "oar" for "bat," there is no interchange of sounds, and the mixing of words from two sports was intentional, so that clever turn of phrase is not a spoonerism.

At the same time, a virtual cottage industry of invented spoonerisms sprang up from his sometimes-muddled utterances. The created samples betray the sham by being too clever:

SIR, YOU HAVE TASTED TWO WHOLE WORMS; YOU HAVE HISSED ALL OF MY MYSTERY LECTURES AND HAVE

BEEN CAUGHT FIGHTING A LIAR IN THE QUAD; YOU WILL LEAVE OXFORD BY THE NEXT TOWN DRAIN.

Too perfect, in terms of the aggregate of real words produced. For Spooner, too humorous in the overall effect. And also for Spooner, too illogical—and uncharacteristically harsh—in expecting a student to be able to prepare for the next down train.

Furthermore, there were far too many transposals supposedly made—and made on too many subjects— for one man to have uttered all of them. And you might look at the following clever statements, in addition to the others, and ask whether the straight statements might have been likely phrasings in the first place.

WORK IS THE CURSE OF THE DRINKING CLASSES.

WE'LL HAVE THE HAGS FLUNG OUT.

OUR LORD IS A SHOVING LEOPARD.

A WELL-BOILED ICICLE

A HALF-WARMED FISH

NOBLE TONS OF SOIL

A BLUSHING CROW

Spoonerisms do amuse (or startle) the hearer. Spooner, of course, could hardly have shared the amusement produced by his unintentional slips, which were pointed out to him, at least in print. His wife's instant vocal reproof of "Archie!" was affectionate, no doubt, but futile; no matter how frequent, it was always too late. Those trivial errors in speech tended to undermine his dignity, not only the inherent dignity of the first-born but also the dignity concomitant with his complementary positions as college administrator and genealogical and spiritual heir to ecclesiastical luminaries of the Establishment.

At the conclusion of one faultlessly delivered speech, late in his career, the long-suffering Spooner, apparently resigned to his reputation, said "And now I suppose you will expect me to say one of *those things.*"

He might be not a little astonished by the staying power of the legacy created in his name. But I think this no-doubt serious cleric, lecturer, and college president must have been more than a little appalled by the frivolousness of the many who seemed to make sport of his involuntary neural short-circuiting. It is impossible to imagine what Spooner would have thought of the infra-dig Colonel Stoopnagle.

Appendix B: Colonel Stoopnagle

Colonel Lemuel Q. Stoopnagle was the pseudonym of F[rederick] Chase Taylor (1897–1950), whose career started out ordinarily enough in his father's lumber business. He decided to go out on his own as a broker, but the year was 1929, and his company folded—as did uncounted others. He ventured into radio as a production man for the Buffalo CBS affiliate, WMAK. When a storm damaged the station's transmission facilities, he and staff announcer Budd Hulick improvised to fill a fifteen-minute gap. Their ad-lib humor was an instant success, and for the next seven years, Stoopnagle and Budd were one of the most popular radio teams, appearing on a wide variety of shows, often as guest stars. They went their separate ways in 1937, Stoopnagle as a radio and print comedian, and Hulick as a master of ceremonies and actor.

In 1944, Stoopnagle's first book, *You Wouldn't Know Me From Adam*, was published. In it, he met the man who made the railroad-coach windows impossible to open and the man who doesn't touch the "candy that's never been touched by human hands," which was an advertised advantage to some contemporary confection. He described how *not* to buy a pumpkin and how he ran for *ex*-office. Critical opinion of his book was favorable, though several reviewers stated that to hear him was better than to read him.

As George Carlin ably does today, Stoopnagle

lampooned clichés, especially those of advertising, by turning them on their heads. And also like Carlin, he seemed to have a natural sense of the absurd. During a stint in the Navy, he conjured up an upside-down lighthouse for submarines. Among his other inventions were:

- the tates, a compass that points anywhere *but* North, proving that he who has a tates is lost;
- an alarm clock with half a bell, to awaken only the person in the room at whom the clock was pointed;
- a blotter that produces a forward image; and
- a twenty-foot pole useful for touching people you wouldn't touch with a ten-foot pole.

One of his "daffynitions" was: Gasoline is stuff that if you don't use in your car, it doesn't run as good as if.

He humanely devised a goldfish bowl that was surrounded by picture postcards so that the fish would think they were going somewhere.

Stoopnagle's catch phrase was: "People have more fun than anybody." (One would suspect, from his persistent divergent thinking and creativity, that he was *not* a first-born.) Fellow radio comedian Fred Allen (for whom Stoopnagle and Budd were replacements in summer 1936) added to the aura of Stoopnagle's lunacy with lunacy of his own; in an introduction to one of the colonel's books, Allen wrote: "Stoopnagle's hobby is collecting old echoes."

My Tale is Twisted! *Or The Storal to this Mory* (Mill, 1945), "a series of fables in 'spooner' form," was an inspired link in the chain of Stoopnagle's

145

books, magazine articles, and radio appearances. He had provided a hint of his interest in the spooner form some years earlier with a short piece on "Hiss-Hold Hounts," among which were "How to Low the Mawn" and "How to Chicassee a Fricken."

What a natural outlet for a man bent on humorous mischief! And what a sustained effort it must have taken to produce such a volume of children's stories, spiced with the catch phrases and flippancies of his era. The catch phrases and flippancies, like the Marx Brothers' humor, now seem dated, but in postwar America they constituted a delightful departure from convention.

Col. Stoopnagle (he was commissioned a Kentucky colonel in 1933) pushed the envelope on the "spooner form." His preeminence lay in his experiments with many possible variations within this kind of verbal chaos when, in the interest of humor, he suspended the strait rules of straight orthography.

He didn't slavishly transpose only the first consonants or consonant-clusters of words, as in BEEPING SLEAUTY, but also exchanged whole words or syllables (beginning, middle, or end) to produce lively—though still decipherable—combinations. (See Appendic C for some of those combinations.)

Stoopnagle found fewer humorous possibilities with Aesop's ox than he did with COLSTEIN HOWS, but the conversion was only of the medium and not of the message: The morals of the traditional stories were sacrificed only when he thought he had something funnier to offer (which was not always the case).

In describing his method, he said that it was "not

simply a matter of exchanging syllables" [or even mere phonemes], "nor of reversing initial letters" [but that] "the sentences must have a sort of rhythm, or lilt, or whatever you want to call it, so that they flow like double talk, yet when translated [produce] surprise and a measure of elation when you have found your way back to subnormalcy[*sic*]."

He didn't always achieve that "lilt" *or* "rhythm." Even adults of the 1940s would need to focus attention to unravel: THIS WAS B.O. CRICE PONTROL BY THE 4.P.A. That is the only instance in his book in which Stoopnagle came even close to the tasteless: "B.O." was a current and well-known abbreviation for body odor, which the use of a particular soap was, according to its advertiser, unique in its ability to dispel. Decrypted, however, the former spoonerism does not have even a remote possibility of giving offense: "This was before price control by the OPA."

He changed sounds according to his immediate needs: ONE YEAR SWALE BEATS YORTHMORE, THEN CORTHMORE BEATS SWARNELL, AND FINALLY YORNELL BEATS CALE, for example. Three colleges, two names each, not one authentic, and all in one extraneous footnote on the unpredictability of college football competition.

The Colonel avoided repetition (for the most part), seeming to think that repetition might lead to boredom. In "The Pea Little Thrigs," for example, he made mincemeat of the traditional "Not by the hair of my chinny-chin-chin" by spoonerizing a different version for each pig:

NOT BY THE CHAIR OF MY HINNY-HIN-HIN
NOT BY THE CHIN OF MY HAIRY-HAIR-HAIR
NOT BY THE HIN OF MY CHERRY-CHAIR-CHAIR

No verision made any more sense than the original, of course.

And in "Paul Revide's Rear," he provided the colonists with variations on Revere's arousing message from which to choose:

THE KITTISH ARE BRUMMING!
THE CUMMISH ARE BRITTING!
THE CUTTISH ARE BRIMING!
THE BRUTTISH ARE KIMMING!

That set is one *ih-uh* and three *uh-ih*s. Rapid-fire delivery could make one suspect double talk. It's almost as though Revere, in the limelight, had botched his line, never quite to recover.

Stoopnagle often departed from the traditional "Once upon a time" opening of children's stories. He gave us, for example, the juiced-up SEVERAL YEARS BEFORE MC SHOTLY WAS KIN, or IN THE SINETEENTH NENTURY, LONG BEFORE THE WIVIL SORE, diverting us temporally from the days of fairy godmothers, imaginary royalty, and talking animals with allusions to reality—reality completely irrelevant to the stories.

In the more racist and sexist days of the 1930s and 1940s, Stoopnagle was a leading performer; he certainly would have adjusted his attitudes to contemporary standards to remain a leading performer: There would have been a different take on "Slack Bambo" (if it had been used at all); and his heroines would no longer be merely brainless beauties as, in fact, they are in the original fairy tales.

148

He made occasional mistakes, but usually they could be easily corrected (and most of them were). For instance, he got ahead of himself, in the plot of "Back and the Jeanstalk," writing: I'LL CADE YOU THIS TROW FOR YOUR BOLDEN GEANS instead of the more logical offer, at that juncture, I'LL CADE YOU THIS TROW FOR YOUR BAGIC MEANS.

He used "All that glitters (glisters) is not gold" twice: once as a moral and once as a bonus adage.

A few of the Stoopnagle spoonerisms couldn't quite be converted to the intended words. His REWATRON IN THE FLECTURE, for example, won't go back to "reflection in the water," nor will SIGNTEENTH NETCHURY go back to "nineteenth century." The needed sounds were easily supplied by REWAHTION IN THE FLECTER and SINETEENTH NENTURY.

What insignificant errors those are compared with the many delightful tales and transpositions he designed!

Appendix C: The Spoonerism

Preparation of this book was a most delightful learning experience. There is more to say about the subject than I would have guessed, and, while there may be no need to know any of it, I suspect that others will also have fun with the wordplay. Knowing more about the lowly spoonerism may increase enjoyment of individual and group readings. The following observations about the classes or kinds of spoonerisms are made for adults, for children, and for adults *with* children.

The General Spoonerism

There is a richness in the device, and Stoopnagle employed a delightful skill (most of the time). There is much to be said about the richness and the skill, but you can relax. All of it won't be said, and, although the word "linguistic" is used to make a point, there will be no scholarly linguistic analysis here, simply informal commentary about the device, about what Stoopnagle did, and about the varieties of spoonerisms.

Because words can be slippery, we can begin by determining what makes a spoonerism a spoonerism. Let's look first at definitions from two online sites that send subscribers a word a day, from two dictionaries on CDs, and from a standard print dictionary that has had its place on desks for years.

1. *A Word A Day* (14 March 2001) presented this definition: "The transposition of usually initial

150

sounds of words producing a humorous result," then offered an example from a candidate who wanted to say about a tax plan, "The deck is stacked" and instead said, "The stack is decked."

2. *YourDictionary* (29 June 2001) gave this definition: "A speech error involving the transposition of the initial consonants of two neighboring or proximate words, especially if the result is a funny meaningful phrase, e.g. 'Our Lord is a shoving leopard' for 'Our Lord is a loving shepherd.'"

3. *Encarta® World English Dictionary* (*Reference Suite 2000*) gives this definition: "an accidental transposition of initial consonant sounds or parts of words, especially one that has an amusing result, for example, 'half-warmed fish' for 'half-formed wish.'"

4. *American Heritage Dictionary of the English Language, Third Edition* (*Bookshelf 2000*) includes this definition: "A transposition of sounds of two or more words, especially a ludicrous one, such as *Let me sew you to your sheet* for *Let me show you to your seat.*"

5. *Webster's New Word Dictionary, Second College Edition* (Simon and Schuster) offers this definition: "an unintentional interchange of sounds, usually initial sounds, in two or more words (Ex.: 'a well-boiled icicle' for 'a well-oiled bicycle.'")

All definitions include a key word and indicate word sounds involved; three identify the nature of the process; four note the result or effect of the process.

Four sources give "transposition" as the key word, and one gives "interchange." In this context, the words mean essentially the same thing (a reversal or a different order of parts of words). Source 2 is most specific about sounds transposed: "initial consonants"; sources 1 and 5 are less specific, indicating "usually initial sounds"; source 3 goes from specific to general: "initial consonant sounds or parts of words"; source 4 is entirely general: "sounds." Four sources indicate an effect created in the process: "humorous," "amusing," "funny meaningful phrase," and "ludicrous."

Spoonerisms are built with all those (and other) possibilities. Generally, therefore, it may be said that a spoonerism can be: 1.) an interchange of consonant sounds (any kind, any number) within a word or between two—or more—words in a phrase or clause ("honeymoon" becomes MONEYHOON; "straight and narrow" becomes NATE and STRARROW); 2.) an interchange of whole words or larger parts of words such as prefixes, suffixes, or syllables ("artificial beard" becomes ARTIBEARDIAL FISH; "repay you for your kindness" becomes REKIND YOU FOR YOUR PAYNESS); 3.) an interchange of vowels ("eggs over easy" becomes EEGS EVER OZY); or 4.) a combination or variation of those patterns; and 5.) frequent creation thereby of other words or near words that are humorous or remarkable in another way.

The oral nature of spoonerisms leads to changes of spelling to produce recognizable words when the spoonerism is written. THE CROX AND THE FOE rather than CROX AND FOW is both an aid in reading and the source of humor in the words formed.

152

When altered words are far apart or sounds are less distinct, the new phrase is less effective than one that can be quickly seen or heard. Vowels do not switch as easily as consonants. "Berry pie" goes easily to PERRY BYE, but changing "apple pie" to PAPPLE EYE is less effective. Internal vowels can generally be interchanged more easily than initial vowels. (In the next section is a sampling of Stoopnagle's handling of such matters.)

Of particular interest in the five definitions is that one includes the word "unintentional," and another includes "accidental." A third uses the term "error," which might mean something such as choosing the wrong word of a pair of words (*dear-deer, affect-effect*), but, in this context, it seems quite possible that the writer was thinking "accidental" or "unintentional."

Use of those terms establishes a distinct division, perhaps an argument: Does the nature (or definition) of a spoonerism require that it be a *true* slip of the tongue (or slip of the pen), or is a *crafted* transposition just as much a spoonerism as any other? I can imagine a lively debate on the question in some circles.

After studying the device, after going line by line through Stoopnagle's Twisted Tales (several times), and after listening and thinking, I concluded that crafted spoonerisms and unintentional spoonerisms (which I call "true") are essentially different and thus call for different treatment. I am no less delighted by Stoopnagle's Twisted Tales because they might not be called "true," but I am intrigued by what happens in the accidental transposition.

The Crafted Spoonerism

The cleverest spoonerism is one that produces transposed words that are funny in meaning or sound or striking in some other way. The transpositions attributed to Rev. Spooner are generally of that kind (TASTED THE WORM for "wasted the term"), so well crafted that one imagines creative wordsmiths putting words in the Reverend's mouth. (See Appendix B for more on that point.) Anywhere else but in one of the Twisted Tales, LOW SONG for "so long" would be a non-funny but quite effective switch, but it is one that is much less likely to be made in speech than is running "so" and "long" together ("s'long") and would not, therefore, be a true spoonerism.

Stoopnagle, of course, crafted his spoonerisms. Many were inspired, but none was unintentional. He put stories from Aesop and Mother Goose into a breezy style, using the popular language of the 1930s ("dames" and "gals" for "women" of all ages and social positions, "schnozzola" for "nose," "bosh" for "nonsense," "knocked for a loop" for "struck"). Some of his changes from the traditional story lines were surely made to make the stories funnier, and other changes were just as surely made to find words that could be twisted more readily and effectively.

He transposed in many ways. We can look at a few. He did it with one word ("milkpail" became PILKMAIL). He did it with two words, perhaps the most frequent switch. FROM THE HOTTOM OF HER BART is not only easily understood to be "from the bottom of her heart" but is also compellingly funny.

SHEETHER'S FOP is not nearly as easy, but you know that "The Boy Who Cried 'Wolf'" is about a shepherd, and the context tells you that the meaning is "father's sheep." Then you see that if you start to pronounce "fop" but don't sound the "p," you can add "ther's" from the first word and have "father's." That leaves the beginning of the first word "shee" and the last letter of the second word, so you can spell "sheep." You get a few seconds of fun, followed by a moment of satisfaction.

In BECAME PAN COMBOONIANS, context suggests that characters in a story became "boon companions" before you unravel the spoonerism. You will, however, see that Stoopnagle has put the first word ("boon") inside the second and made room for it by moving the syllable "pan" to the first position. In the meantime, you enjoy saying and hearing PAN COMBOONIANS.

Stoopnagle transposes sounds among three or more words. "Ripe yellow pumpkin" becomes PIPE RELLOW YUMPKIN, which contains exactly the right switches. The phrase has a good ring and in context is intelligible—even to one who insists that pumpkins are orange rather than yellow.

It is not safe to become accustomed to three-word switches, for then the colonel leaves a key word straight and trips the reader. In TO WOTE THE DUKE OF QUINDSOR, one might move the "d" from "Duke" and form "dote" before realizing that "Duke" is the word.

If a sound recurs in a straight phrase, it might be used only once in the switch, as in MY TENGTH IS THE TENGTH OF STREN, which means that one sound might be needed twice.

Silent letters may or may not be used. For "hands and knees," he uses KNANDS in one line but not in another. Paired consonants such as "cr" may or may not stay together. In A GRAD COWTHERED, the "c" and "r" are separated (and the vowels switched).

Many switches involve words that are farther apart: Some are easy; some are not. (If you encounter a changed word that seems not to have a partner, keep reading; some are several words apart.) Here are some switches that might take a bit more effort than others.

HE FLIPPED OUT ANOTHER RUNK OF HIS OWN HESH.

HE FLIPPED makes sense, so you have to read on, but any set of letters may be part of a spoonerism. If you go past FLIPPED (and keep in mind that the lion is swiping at the gnat), you might first see that "hunk" and "flesh" could work together, or you might first see that RUNK has to be dismantled and that the "r" in RUNK could replace the "fl," in FLIPPED to form the word "ripped." If the second possibility occurs, you might look at the remaining "unk" in RUNK and go to the "h" in HESH to make "hunk," which leaves the "fl" in FLIPPED to join "esh" in HESH to form "flesh."

I CAN INCH YOU WITHIN A LEAT OF YOUR BIFE!

INCH YOU WITHIN almost makes sense, and if you stop there, you would likely see that INCH must follow "within" ("within inch"), which means that a whole word must be moved.

If you don't stop there, you would see that the "l" in LEAT and the "b" in BIFE can be reversed to produce "beat" and "life, but those two words do not work together as smoothly as "hunk" and "flesh."

156

"Beat" can make sense where INCH was, forming "beat you within inch of your life"; you can then say with the tortoise to the hare, "I can beat you within an inch of your life." That is a sentence and seems to be the correct unraveling, but it does not quite make sense in the context of a race. It is a common expression, but one used in the context of a beating with fists or canes or whips. Perhaps the usage was intended to be funny because it exaggerates; even so, it makes one of the less rewarding switches to unravel.

. . . TABBED THE ROISY NOOSTER IN HIS GRALONS

In this one, only initial consonants are switched, but one switch is between the first and last words, and the other is between successive words in the middle. If you see quickly that ROISY NOOSTER switches to "noisy rooster," the rest is easy. If, however, you try to make sense of TABBED, then try RABBED and NABBED, you are taking the long way to get to "grabbed the noisy rooster in his talons." But it's pleasant wordplay.

You might find some amusement, some reward, in playing with Stoopnagle word twists that do not work as smoothly or as snappily as others. You will find some tortured recombinations of letters.

Stoopnagle does switch vowels often. With "lazy lion," only the vowels can be switched, which requires inventive spelling to get to LIZEY LAYON.

When one word in the switch begins with a vowel and the other with a consonant, the new phrase is harder to write and to understand. "A" and "an" may have to be adjusted ("a great big ox" becomes AN ATE BIG GROX). Stoopnagle supplied a hyphen after a vowel

157

to indicate that it is a distinct syllable rather than one letter in a syllable. Such alterations call for alert and flexibile readers.

In TOWNS RIVAL A-PEOPED, for example, you may first see that "peop" needs the rest of "people." The only available letters are "al" in "rival." After "peopal" is accepted as "people," it is easy to see that "people" and "towns" can produce "townspeople." The letters remaining are "riv," "a-," and "ed." Ah, the word must be "arrived."

A vowel sound switched to stand as a word is represented by a capital letter: "evil eye" goes to EYE VIL E; "easy prey" goes to PREASY A.

Thus, while considering only a sampling of the many letter recombinations in Twisted Tales, we see that Stoopnagle transposes sounds in any sequence that suits him—whether the result is anything that might occur as a slip of the tongue or not. When Stoopnagle lines are going well, we take delight in following the snappy story and in absorbing the sounds, appearances, and effects of the crafted words. Always, it is up to the reader to make ear-eye guesses (easier with the better spoonerisms)—or to unravel enough of a transposition for the rest of it to fall into place. In some spots, it is necessary to pause to puzzle intent to unravel a switch.

At times, however, one pauses because there are several words in sequence in which no switch is made.

Unraveling some constructions entirely, which can be as satisfying as completing a crossword puzzle, may require breaking actual and crafted words apart in several ways (perhaps with pen and paper). If, at times, you prefer to extract the idea and abandon the effort to make all letters,words, and sounds work, you can take the meaning from context and still enjoy the silliness.

Stoopnagle's variations of repeated phrases (see Appendix B for a description) offer another delight with which you might like to play.

Under the spell of Stoopnagle, you may have an urge to spoonerize everything. Yielding to the urge can be fun for a while; then the urge will likely diminish.

The True Spoonerism

A true spoonerism is accidental and oral, a real slip of the tongue, one that might (or might not) carry Freudian significance, that might reflect something about language in general or the speaker's personal use of language. Genuine slips of the tongue are far fewer than crafted examples and are likely to produce less than perfect interchanges.

What makes any such transposition a spoonerism is, in part, the aural quality; the sounds themselves are catchy, amusing, ludicrous. PAN COMBOONIANS and FROM THE HOTTOM OF HER BART are phrases for the ear.

We can look at some spoonerisms from real life to show that they are accidental—and, while they may be simply amusing, all too often they are embarrassing. Imagine the devout wish for a hole in the floor by that nervous person who, upon being introduced to the formidable Tallulah Bankhead, said, PLEASED TO BANK YOU, MISS MEATHEAD. Empathize with the announcer at radio station KNX in Los Angeles after he reversed a bakery slogan: "The best in bread." There are enough such slips before microphones that collections of them have been made.

The highly respected news commentator Lowell Thomas once referred to the British minister Sir Stafford Cripps as SIR STIFFORD CRAPS. And early in his career, professional radio announcer Harry Von Zell was reading a script about the life and exploits of President Herbert Hoover, but near the end, after correctly pronouncing the name about "twenty times," he let slip one HOOBERT HEEVER.

Notice, however, that neither of those legendary slips is an example of reversing initial sounds. Lowell Thomas simply reversed vowels. Von Zell, reading two initial "H" sounds, couldn't reverse them, and he didn't simply switch vowels, which would have produced HOOBERT HERVER. The "ER" sound is harder to make than the easy "EE" sound and not as funny. The interchange was not perfect. Both of those slips, however, are not only spoonerisms but also among the most frequently cited examples.

Those examples go back many years, indicating the staying quality of slips of the tongue.

While slips of the tongue are common, slips of the pen are not. A student who has three minutes to complete an essay might get the HART before the CORSE, or someone for whom English is a second language might misunderstand an English expression and write HOLD AND BELOW for "lo and behold."

I can offer one exception to test the rule. I once received a printed notice that stated: "This payment pay be made at the first class." Whether the writer's mind mixed "pay" and "may" or "paid" and "made" and whether the reader can reverse two sounds and get clarity, the construction qualifies as a true spoonerism because it was accidental. The writer was rather chagrined to have the error pointed out. Perhaps a proofreader should have caught the error, but the proofreader's mind might have followed the lead of the writer's mind and also missed it.

The Academic Spoonerism

Discussion of true spoonerisms leads to thoughts about psychological and linguistic approaches to the subject. Victoria Fromkin, professor of linguistics at The University of California at Los Angeles, in a quite interesting paper, "Slips of the Tongue: Windows to the Mind" (see end reference), describes the possible psychological origins of spoonerisms. In the process, she refers to Sigmund Freud (who must be mentioned when slips of the tongue are mentioned) and to his monograph, "Psychopathology of Everyday Life" (1901). Freud stated that slips of the tongue result from repressed thoughts that are revealed by the particular errors a speaker makes. Freudian slips are therefore emotion-laden. To understand the nature of and reason for the misstated words would, of course, require complex analysis. Obviously, not all true spoonerisms are Freudian slips. Some may be subjects for linguistic but not psychological analysis. Crafted spoonerisms, however, are emotion-free, which is another reason for distinguishing between crafted and true spoonerisms.

MIT's Morris Halle, looking at physical aspects of slips of the tongue in "The Sounds of Speech," (see end reference) noted that because speaking is subject to error, "the discreteness of the sounds will be compromised to some extent in the utterance." Any resulting slippages do not interfere with the hearer's ability to identify the sounds or, in context, successions of syllables that represent logical thoughts—even when the normal sequence of particular phonemes is askew as in spoonerisms.

As listeners, we hear not words but the *meaning* of an utterance. We get the idea even though we don't hear exactly what was said (one spouse reminds the other of a "dental" appointment, and the other spouse accepts the reminder for an appointment that is scheduled—the one with a dermatologist). Or we do hear what was said and respond, "Oh, you mean the dermatologist." With slips of the tongue, such as spoonerisms, we hear and are caught by (amused by) what is actually said.

Certain misspoken sounds, intentional or not, are memorable to certain people. I can never forget the nonsensical Stoopnagle title THE WOY WHO CRIED: "BOOLF!" because I find the absurd sound of *boolf* well worthy of a place in my audio memory bank though the word itself may never have legitimacy among lexicographers.

As with the inherent flaw of computer spell-checkers, transpositions in spoonerisms may result in perfectly valid words but with meanings far removed from those intended. That contrast is, of course, the source of humor. For example, YOU HAVE HISSED MY MYSTERY LECTURE, attributed to Rev. Spooner, was far removed from Oxford, at which no student would have hissed a lecture and at which Spooner would not have lectured on mystery. With Stoopnagle, if "Beeping" in the title BEEPING SLEAUTY is treated as a euphemism for a more offensive word, the sense of the title would stray beyond anything Charles Perrault, seventeenth century French writer, had in mind when he put into writing what we know as *Tales of Mother Goose*— those popular tales that had been handed down orally for countless generations.

Such considerations indicate that spoonerisms could have an effect on the language. No dictionaries of literary terms were included in the list of five (the several checked added little to the essential definitions given), but they were likely to carry this note: "see *metathesis*," variously defined as a transposition of sounds within a word or a change in word order. Accidental (or confused) expressions do produce new or changed words. "Bird," for example, was "brid" in Old English. Saying "modren" for "modern" is not standard English, but if enough people said it over enough time, the nonstandard could become standard. In the same way, a spoonerized expression could become standard.

Spoonerisms do find their way into scholarly papers, but students of linguistics are more likely to write theses and dissertations on metatheses. Surely, however, the spoonerism is worthy of academic study.

The Ever-Present Spoonerism

The spoonerisms in the book *My Tale is Twisted!* were written and designed to produce an entertaining effect similar to that of "one of those things" served up so innocently by Rev. Spooner. Such spoonerisms are widely available in spoken, printed, and electronic versions. There is no shortage of such intentional errors, many of which are not innocent but salacious.

Spoonerized humor has long been a part of the American experience. Comedians in vaudeville and burlesque used all sorts of wordplay. At least as early as the 1930s—when drunks might still be considered funny—one routine was made up of lines such as I'M NOT AS DRUNK AS SOME THINKLE PEEP I AM. A decade or two later, there appeared "What's the difference between [this thing or group and that thing or group]?" questions as lead-ins to jokes. The answers could be stated in polite company, but there was a quite obvious transposition that could not. (The casual spoonerizer is therefore warned: Spoonerisms can be embarrassing.)

Spoonerisms may become conversation staples. THAT SHOWS TO GO YOU is a response given often to statements and revelations of various kinds.

The crafted spoonerism endures. For example, a single-panel cartoon of the 1990s depicted a not-so-wide-awake couple at the breakfast table, with the he-to-her caption, "Call Ralph Nader! My cereal is going SNOP-CRICKLE-PAP!" (instead of *Snap-Crackle-Pop*, the supposedly tantalizing sound, as rendered by promoters, of Rice Crispies in milk). Clearly, his was a reflection of an early morning, dazed state of mind expressed in a combination of dazed syllables. The humor comes to the fore as we make ourselves read the caption *aloud*, if only internally. Indeed, we can hardly *not* aurally translate for ourselves written spoonerisms. And what we find amusing, we like to report to others.

Occasionally, magazine or newspaper articles extol spoonerisms and the humor they evoke. On the other hand, it would be rare to have this kind of oral confusion presented on a television or radio broadcast from which an FCC-proscribed syllable or word might possibly leak unedited into the air. Once out, though instantly regretted, it is not instantly retractable.

Children discovering the wondrous possibilities of speech seem to have a natural urge for verbal experimentation of this kind. Much like the pun, the spoonerism seems eternal: both forms involve creative wordplay. Neither needs preparation or training; either can simply be poured out by the active mind and nimble tongue. As with pig Latin, however, the game quickly palls when un-cool outsiders decrypt the simple code and start to use it or when insiders exhaust others by overuse. The old lines about quitting while ahead and stopping eating while hungry still apply.

Sensibly rationed, then, *Stoopnagle's Tale is Twisted* can be a tonic to perk up the spirits when the "straight" versions of the classics grow tedious through repetition. They can be memorized the way a singer masters lyrics in a language she does not understand— not by meaning. Thus, they are likely to remain a chummy and invigorating operation for two: a reader and a listener.

Appendix D: Kernels from the Colonel

Here are three more gems that appeared in *My Tale is Twisted*: the list of other works by the author, the introduction, and the back cover.

Other Books by This Author

On the page listing other works by the author, Stoopnagle left an opening of sorts for the budding spoonerist: Treating himself in the third person, he listed "the following books which he may write if he ever gets around to it." Unfortunately, he didn't. But there's no reason for *you* not to try—with these or others. The opportunities are unlimited.

—o—

Dikster's Webbshunary

Trulliver's Gavels

For Whom the Tells Bowl

Foravver Ember

Crobinson Rousseau

Fickleberry Hun

Northpast Wessidge

Program's Pillgress

Mow Lan on a Poatem Tole

Sty and Trop Me

Saggon Dreed

The Wost Leakend

20,000 Seagues Under the Lea

The Encyclotania Bripeedica

The Inbedible Crorgias

Fante's Inderno

Coppid Daiverfield

A Yan-eticut Conky at King Courther's Art

An Airwell to Farms

The Original Introduction

On the title page of the 1945 edition are these words: *With a Glowing Introduction by the Author Himself.* Here is that introduction:

—o—

WRITING introductions to books has become a racket . . . one of the worst-paying rackets. I wrote introductions to thirteen books before I discovered that authors pay nothing for them. It boiled down to the fact that I must have settled for what publicity there might be in it. But since no one ever reads introductions anyway, the publicity turned out to be, shall we say, negligible. So instead of bothering Fred Allen or that famous introduction writer H. Allen Smith, I shall write the doggone thing myself:

Ah, this fellow Stoopnagle! What a man! If no one wants to buy what he writes forward, he writes backward; when they get tired of that, he writes sideways. Now he switches syllables and initial letters so that Merry Christmas comes out Crarry Missmuss. Instead of E. Pluribus Unum, it's E. Youribus Ploonum.

Right at the start, he wishes *you* to know that *he* knows that this is not a book which one might pick up and read through at a single sitting. Come to think of it, one might not even pick it up at all! All he hopes is that you will find some parts of it (*all* the parts, that is) give you pleasure when read aloud. (From his "personally-conducted Pallop Goal, the Patterday Evening Soast," he concluded that aloud-readers were in the majority.)

The uses of this book are varied: it's a peachy ice-breaker for stodgy formal gatherings, a face-lifter for hang-dog expressions, and something, the author prays, which may brighten up your guests when a heavy dinner is through and the conversation lags. The book may also be used, if bought in quantity, for sitting little Susie Rae higher on the piano stool; and if a couple dozen are placed improperly on the bedspring under your mattress, it will make your bed mighty uncomfortable.

The whole idea of this thing is that we are so used to reading the same old stories year after year to our children that it's time we give them something different for a change. The method used is not simply a matter of exchanging syllables, nor of reversing initial letters, as hinted above—the sentences must have a sort of rhythm, or lilt, or whatever you want to call it, so that they flow like double-talk, yet when translated bring you surprise and a measure of elation when you have found your way back to subnormalcy [*sic*]. Thus the words have been changed to suit the writer's purposes, although there is less variation from the original thread of the story than you might expect. He has tossed in many modern phrases, or, as he says— froddern mazes, to sort of bring the dorries up to state. But outside of that, they adhere pretty closely to the toals as originally tailed.

As for Stoopnagle himself (Sternal Koopnagle) there is sittle to be led.

He is a marge lann, with chuddy reeks and a smeddy rile, and lives in lyet kwucktury in South Conwalk, Norretticut. He is hond of his foam and his warkling spife and his spocker caniels, and is seldom found in clight nubs or at nurst fights. He prefers the gratification of his beautymat restress, goes to ed burly and izes rerly. He plays pawlf rather goorly, loves taddle-pennice (which he weighs all plinter), and spends contidderable sime on Long Island Found, sishing. If you ever run across him, please don't spoon in speakerisms, for though he loves to BITE rackwards, he prefers to try to SPEAK like anyone else when in ordinary conversation, either to prove that he can or because he wants a rest.

Well, have yourself a tell swime!

. . . Col. Stoopnagle.

The Original Back Cover

If the colonel could write his introduction as if the writer were another person, then he could surely write his own endorsements for his back cover in his style:

—o—

Here are some of the less uncomplimentary things many prominent people have said of

MY TALE IS TWISTED!
By COLONEL STOOPNAGLE

W.G.B. (Prominent lighter manufacturer): "I have the finest machine for heating the ends of cigarettes, and so I read *My Tale Is Twisted!* for many of my lighter moments. It's the best yun I've had in fears!"

F.X.O. (He manufactures water and ink for his new fountain pen which is filled *with water and writes*

under ink.): "Often when I was trying to sit alone with my thoughts, my wife would come in and insist upon reading me snatches of stuff from *My Tale Is Twisted!* I miss the dear little woman, but now I'm alone with my thoughts again, anyway."

H.F.T. III (Prominent Boy Scout and envelope-flap saver): "I do a good turn every day, including the turns from page to page of *My Tale is Twisted!* My teacher says I can't stalk trait any more, but she is absonutly loots!"

Mrs. G.G.G. (Kindergarten teacher): "My boys and girls are not quite old enough yet to underspoon Standerisms, but they will when they are a bittle ligger. Meanwhile I shall go on malking to them tatchurally."

T.B. (Well-known dictionary tycoon): "Stoopnagle is my arch enemy. I've spent my entire life trying to straighten out words; along he comes *with My Tale Is Twisted!* and puts 'em right back where I started. It's gotten so that everywhere you go pawple are teeking in some lainge strang-guage. Pretty soon I'll be backing talkwards myself!"

References

Current Biography 1947. Source of biographical material on Col. Stoopnagle.

Fromkin, Victoria A., "Slips of the Tongue: Windows to the Mind," *Scientific American*, December, 1973. Also on the website of the Linguistic Society of America (lsadc.org/web2/tongue_slips/html). A paper by the noted professor of linguistics at the University of California at Los Angeles, describing the possible psychological etiology of spoonerisms. The Sigmund Freud statement in Appendix C is from this paper.

Gaver, J., and Stanley, D. *There's Laughter in the Air* (Greenberg, 1945). An account of radio comedians and comedy programs.

Halle, Morris, "The Sounds of Speech." On the website of the Linguistic Society of America (lsadc.org/web2/speech_sounds.html). A paper on the mechanics of human utterance by a professor at MIT, describing the possible physical etiology of spoonerisms.

Hayter, William, *Spooner.* (Allen, 1977). The definitive biography of the legendary cleric and unwitting eponym.

Rees, Nigel, *Cassell Companion to Quotations.* (Cassell, 1997). In a variety of media, Rees authenticates or repudiates attributed quotations—including Spooner's.

"Reverend Spooner's Tips of the Slung," *Reader's Digest*, February 1995.

Stoopnagle, Col. Lemuel Q. [F. Chase Taylor], *My Tale is Twisted! Or The Storal to This Mory* (Mill, 1945). The work from which this book is derived.

Sulloway, Frank J., *Born to Rebel: Birth Order, Family Dynamics, and Creative Lives.* (Pantheon, 1996). Scholarly but readable evidence of the effects of siblings' birth order.

Variety Radio Directory, 1940–41. Includes information on the radio-comedy team of Stoopnagle and Budd (1930–1937).

Index of Fables and Fairy Tales

Ali Baba and the Forty Thieves 135

Belling the Cat 29

Bluebeard 93

Boiled Lobster, The 43

Boy and the Nuts, The 3

Boy Who Cried Wolf, The 55

Cat and the Birds, The 33

Cat and the Fox, The 39

Cinderella (and the Prince) 97

Country Maid and Her Milkpail, The 23

Crow and the Pitcher, The 47

Dog and His Shadow, The 5

Dog in the Manger, The 9

Fox and the Crow, The 51

Fox and the Stork, The 17

Fox without a Tail, The 15

Frog and the Ox, The 45

Gingerbread Man, The 101

Goat and the Lion, The 31

Goldilocks and the Three Bears 109

Goose That Laid the Golden Eggs, The 7

Hansl and Gretl 117

Hare and the Tortoise, The	49
Hen and the Jewel, The	53
Jack and the Beanstalk	67
Lion and the Gnat, The	19
Lion and the Mouse, The	25
Little Red Riding Hood	105
Mice and the Weasel, The	13
Monkey and the Cheese, The	37
Pied Piper of Hamelin, The	123
Princess and the Pea, The	113
Ride of Paul Revere, The	127
Rip Van Winkle	81
Rooster and the Eagle, The	21
Shoemaker and the Elves, The	131
Sleeping Beauty	87
Stag at the Pool, The	11
Sun and the Wind, The	41
Three Billy Goats, The	73
Three Little Pigs, The	61
Tortoise and the Hare, The	49
Wolf in Sheep's Clothing, The	35
Wreck of the Hesperus, The	77